Leonita froze in mid-step, her head swiveling until her eyes caught Carter's.

"Get back," he hissed, then lurched to one of the windows.

Cautiously he curled back a corner of the burlap and peered over the edge.

Jorge, Leonita's brother, lay on the very edge of the trees about twenty yards from the house with his head spread all over the ground nearby.

"What is it? Is it Jorge . . . ?"

She was at his shoulder, her hands like a vise around his bicep.

"Yes. He's dead, Leonita . . . and in not a very pretty way."

If Carter expected wailing and hysterics, he got none. A few mumbled words that sounded like a prayer formed on her lips, and then she raised her head to stare at Carter. Her eyes were clear and dry.

"What are we to do?" Leonita asked.

"Stay alive . . ."

NICK CARTER IS IT!

FROM THE NICK CARTER
KILLMASTER SERIES

NICK CARTER

KILLMASTER

THE ALGARVE AFFAIR

C

CHARTER BOOKS, NEW YORK

THE ALGARVE AFFAIR

A Charter Book/published by arrangement with
The Condé Nast Publications, Inc.

PRINTING HISTORY
Charter Original/February 1984

ISBN: 0-441-01276-0

Charter Books are published by The Berkley Publishing Group,
200 Madison Avenue, New York, New York 10016.
PRINTED IN THE UNITED STATES OF AMERICA

*Dedicated to the men of the
Secret Services of the
United States of America*

ONE

A misty rain seemed to hover in the air around Nick Carter's head rather than fall to the cobblestones beneath his feet. His heels made a clicking sound that bounced off the brightly colored *azulejos*, the tiles that covered the façades of the houses he passed.

He had carefully followed, down to the last detail, the driver's directions since leaving the cab on a larger, main thoroughfare. Now, ten minutes into the Alfama, the old Arab quarter of Lisbon, Carter was pretty sure he was lost.

It was easy to do. The streets were modeled after the casbahs of Morocco and Algeria—all of six feet wide and curling like a hundred serpents through the quarter.

Noise and slightly brighter lights to his right drew him in that direction. There were two neon signs. Both were late-night clubs, but neither of them filled the bill.

A small girl with an elfin face and hair the color of tar lounged against the wall near one of the clubs. She was wrapped in a black raincoat two sizes two large for her, and bright eyes like two chunks of coal peeked from beneath a black shawl.

"*Boa noite . . . por favor . . .*"

"*Sim?*" she replied, her eyes registering Carter from

1

the knit cap on his head over the stubbly-bearded face to
his pea jacket and jeans.

"Onde está O Bistro?"

"O Bistro . . ." She thought for a second, then began
rattling off directions to the club in rapid-fire Portuguese.

"Devagar . . . devagar," Carter said, holding his
hands up, palms out, as he asked her to slow down.

Suddenly she recognized the accent. *"Inglês?"*

"Sim," Carter nodded. *"Fala inglês?"*

"A little. Go down to second turn . . . this way."

"Right?"

"Sim. Then go to end that street and right again. You
will see sign."

"Obrigado . . . adeus." Carter started to move away,
but her voice halted him.

"Sailor?" Carter nodded. "You go hear fado?"

"Sim. Why?"

"Not too many sailors like to hear fado singing . . .
boring. What you do after fado?"

"Get drunk maybe. Why?"

"You want some fushy-fushy after fado, sailor, I still
be here."

"Fushy-fushy?" Carter said, and then he smiled. One
way or another, it was called the same the world over. He
fished several twenty-five escudo coins from his pocket
and pressed them into her hand. "Maybe some other
night. Tonight I want to feel sad."

The girl shrugged and Carter moved on. He made the
turns as per her instructions, and minutes later he found
himself under a small swinging sign. O Bistro, in red
letters, was illuminated by a bare yellow bulb.

One look both ways told him the street was empty.

"Boa noite, senhor. A table?"

Carter nodded and followed the waiter. When he saw
that he was being taken down front near the stage, he
grasped the man's arm.

"Não," Carter said and motioned to a table toward the rear in a nearly dark corner.

"But, *senhor,* that table is for three."

"I'll drink enough for three," Carter replied. *"Porto, por favor."*

"Sim, senhor."

Carter eased his long, lean, and tired body into the wicker chair against the wall and dropped cigarettes and lighter on the tiny table.

He had gotten no sleep on the flight from New York, and precious little more than a catnap since touchdown at 6:30 that morning. After checking into the Lisboa Plaza, he had grabbed a quick shower and then followed instructions by letting Portuguese internal security know he was in the country.

As an AXE agent, this was a rare *modus operandi,* but then this entire mission was a bit off the beaten path for a Killmaster.

The head of Portuguese security was Miguel Avila, a short, dapper man with the piercing eyes of a customs agent and a perfect command of English.

This was good. Carter was fluent in several languages, but Portuguese wasn't one of them. The frequent *"zhhh's"* in the language, which sounded to him like a tide rolling over rocks, constantly threw him.

"I have instructions from NATO command, Senhor Carter, to keep hands off while you are in my country. You are to have a free rein."

"I appreciate that."

"I will expect, however, that you will keep me informed of your progress. When the time comes for an arrest, then we will step in."

Carter suppressed a smile. Miguel Avila had received instructions from Washington through NATO, but not knowledge of just what kind of agent Nick Carter was. With any luck there would be no arrest.

Carter's orders from David Hawk, head of AXE, were to remove the head or heads of this operation. Permanently.

The waiter was merely a shadow as he deposited a carafe of port, one glass, and a check on the table in passing.

Carter poured, then lit a cigarette. Over the rim of the glass and through the spiraling smoke, he perused his fellow patrons. Down front were the tourists: giggly ladies and bored, paunchy men on package tours from the States and the U.K.

In the middle of the room was the younger set. Fado was a fairly cheap date and still good entertainment. Along the back wall were the real aficionados, the native men and women who lived and breathed fado. Carter guessed that most of these, if not all, were regulars to O Bistro or any of the other tiny restaurants that featured the traditional art form.

One by one, Carter checked the men out. Most were dressed cheaply in the traditional black that seemed part of the Portuguese soul. A few wore work clothes, jackets with blue shirts and no ties.

Only one, a greasy little man with a thin mustache seated near the door, might fit the bill: doper, smuggler, killer. His clothes were a little sharper than the others. Carter noticed little things; the tie he wore matched his suit, and the cuffs of his white shirt weren't frayed.

Like Carter, the little man was casing the others in the room. When their eyes met and the other man flinched ever so slightly, Carter made a mental note to keep one eye over his shoulder when he left.

The dimming lights and the sound of a guitar being tuned shifted his attention to the small stage. In no time the guitarist was ready and joined by a Portuguese viola that looked like a large mandolin.

By the time the lights had faded and the entire room was

bathed in just flickering candlelight, the musicians had already gotten up a good head of steam.

Then a narrow spotlight shaded with a smoky lens came on, and the *fadista* stepped from the shadows. She was dressed all in black, with a black shawl over her dark head. Her face was both haunted and beautiful at the same time, with strikingly black eyes and high, chiseled cheekbones.

Around him Carter heard little gasps, awe-filled sighs, and her name, Leonita, whispered reverently.

Slowly, as she haughtily surveyed her audience, she tightened the shawl around her shoulders and clasped it with both hands between her breasts. Then the eyes, black as night, closed. The head went back, the heavily glossed lips parted, and she began to sing.

For the next hour she sang the sad songs of the fado, songs of pain remembered and yet to come.

Loosely interpreted, fado means fate, and to the Portuguese fate would always imply sadness and pain.

Leonita Silva didn't sing of her fate simply from her chest, her throat, or her lips. She sang from her soul.

At the end of the hour, when she faded back into the shadows, the women in the audience were weeping, the men were awestruck, and the aficionados were nodding, their way of acknowledging her greatness.

It took several minutes for the aura of the fado to dissipate from the room. When it did, the clinking of glasses and the chatter seemed more subdued.

Slowly the waiters began moving through the crowd with several albums made by Leonita in her career. Leonita herself appeared from behind a black curtain in the rear and moved from table to table signing the album covers. At each table she would sit a few moments to chat.

Carter bought an album and waited.

"Would you like my record autographed, *senhor?*"

Up close she was even more mysteriously beautiful.

The eyes seemed even darker, and their brilliance more penetrating. In the softer candlelight her features were not so harsh, but they were still defined and strong.

"Yes, I would . . . very much."

As if she had willed her legs to melt, she slipped into the chair opposite Carter in one fluid movement, reaching for the album at the same time.

"You enjoy the fado?"

"I do. It has always spoken to my soul, but never so much as tonight."

"*Obrigado, senhor . . .*"

"Please inscribe it 'To Nick . . . whose time has come.' "

Her head was bent, but Carter could still see her eyes when they rolled upward to meet his. He also saw the slight quiver in her hand when the felt tip began to move over the album cover.

"When did you arrive in Lisbon?" she asked in English, her lips barely moving, her voice a whisper.

"This morning . . . TWA from New York," he replied, masking his own lips with a cigarette between two fingers.

"And before New York?"

"Arlington . . . Washington."

"And the money?"

"I have it with me."

"Any objections to this evening?"

"None."

Her face was impassive, the barest suggestion of a smile at one corner of her mouth when she raised her head and handed him the album. When she spoke again in Portuguese, her voice was raised so that any around them, who cared, could hear her words.

"I hope you enjoy the record, *senhor.*"

"*Obrigado.*"

Carter killed about twenty minutes smoking, sipping his port, and watching her move the rest of the way around the room before he turned the album cover over and read what she had written.

The Castelo de São Jorge in two hours' time. Near the old cannons on the outer ramparts. I am being watched. Beware that you are not followed. Bring a car.

The old castle was perched on the highest of Lisbon's seven hills, just above the Alfama. Carter was fairly sure he knew the place on the ramparts she meant.

He checked his watch. It was 1:30. There would be just enough time to get back to the hotel, pick up his rented Seat, and drive up the hill to the Castelo de São Jorge.

He dropped more than enough escudos on the table to cover the bill and, with the album under his arm, headed for the door.

It didn't dawn on Carter until he hit the street that the greasy little man who had been sitting by the door had already left.

It had all started with a very angry phone call from a very exasperated Ginger Bateman.

"Where the hell have you been, Nick? I've been calling every pub, saloon, and scrounge hangout in Washington!"

"Then I don't know why you couldn't get me. I've been in every one of them."

"Are you sober?"

"No. Should I be? . . . I mean, it's my last night in town, it's Mexico City in the morning . . ."

"No, it isn't," she replied in a lower tone, one that was more in keeping with the secretary and good right arm of David Hawk, head of AXE.

"Who says?"

"The man says."

"Hawk?"

"Is there any other man? Can you be at the Circle in an hour?"

Dupont Circle was the headquarters for the Amalga-

mated Press and Wire Services. Behind AP&WS, read
AXE.

Carter looked through the phone booth glass at the
leggy blonde with the huge, luminous eyes and the incred-
ibly well-filled blouse, and sighed. Her name was Adele,
she was twenty-eight years old, and she had been in
Washington for three days. She had come to Washington
for two reasons: to work in her daddy's office—her daddy
was a Congressman—and to raise all the hell she could.

Nick Carter was the first man she had met in
Washington.

He sighed again.

"Well?" Ginger demanded.

"Can we make it *two* hours?"

"An hour and a half. This is hot. You're on the midnight TWA out of Kennedy for Lisbon."

"Right. *Ciao!*"

Carter dropped the receiver back on its cradle and
headed for the bar.

"Adele . . ."

"You know, Nick, I think you're right."

"About what?"

"I *am* tired of barhopping. Let's go back to your place
and have a nightcap."

"Oh, my God."

Carter explained in quick staccato sentences that Amalgamated Press and Wire Services had a hot story brewing
in the Far East. He had to catch a plane right away, etc.,
etc., etc., and other ridiculous explanations that, even to
him, began to sound ludicrous by the time he was backing
toward the door.

Over his shoulder he saw Adele already casting her eyes
around the crowded lounge for his replacement.

"Damn," he murmured under his breath, his mind
conjuring up images of the hell she was going to raise
without him.

He hailed a cab, gave the driver his address, and settled

back to contemplate the change in missions. He had been looking forward to Mexico City. It was to have been a routine surveillance mission on a couple of KGB types recruiting through the Soviet embassy there.

Now it was Portugal, and fast. Ginger had said it was hot. That meant unlimbering his pet Lugar, Wilhelmina, and honing up the stiletto, Hugo, that had saved his skin so many times in the past by rupturing others.

Well, so be it. He had had it easy for three months now, routine missions with no reason to exercise his Killmaster designation.

When Bateman said "hot," it usually meant a wet run.

An execution. An elimination.

No big deal, just a job. Everybody has to make a living. For Nick Carter, living often meant killing. Not that he enjoyed it. He just didn't think about it.

Since the beginning of time there had been the good guys and the bad guys.

Carter considered himself one of the good guys.

The top condo of an Arlington highrise was home for about three months out of the year. Home for Nick Carter was little more than a place to unwind between missions and a drop-off for extra clothes.

It took him less than a half hour to pack, and forty minutes later he was walking into the oak-paneled inner sanctum of David Hawk.

"Sit, N3," growled the big man from behind a cloud of rancid cigar smoke, "and do a quick read on this."

He dropped a thin manila folder into Carter's lap and moved like an aging cat over the room's deep pile carpet toward a bar.

"Drink?"

"I've had enough," Carter replied, opening the folder.

"I heard," Hawk said, adding a chuckle. "Sorry about Adele."

Carter grinned himself. He had known Adele for twenty-four hours. Hawk had probably known about

Adele ten minutes after Carter had met her.

It was the way of it. Hawk knew every move his people made. That was why AXE had survived congressional hearings, political infighting, and budget cuts.

Hawk knew everything.

Carter didn't mind. It came with the territory.

The folder contained a mission progress report from Commander Ramon Alvarez, U.S.N., on special assignment to SHAPE, Supreme Headquarters Allied Powers Europe. It had been sent two weeks earlier to SHAPE, outside Brussels, then forwarded to NATO and to the Pentagon.

Carter's eyes flew down the pages, easily digesting what he read and filling in a lot of blanks with what he knew about procedure.

The gist of the report was that Alvarez had established proof that there was in existence a huge drug-growing, -refining, and -smuggling operation operating between North Africa and Portugal.

The opium poppies were grown and harvested in Angola. From there they were being shipped to Algeria for processing. The raw opium was then shipped across the Mediterranean in tramp steamers, where it was picked up at sea by fishing boats and smuggled into various villages along the southern coast of Portugal, the Algarve.

There it was cut and set up for reshipment throughout Europe.

Most of this looked pretty routine to Carter, not much more than a well-organized, big-time doper operation, except for the next-to-last notation by Commander Alvarez.

. . . HAVE PHOTO, VISUAL, AND WORD-OF-MOUTH PROOF THAT MARIA CHANETTE, AKA COCO CHANETTE, IS HEAD OF THE NORTH AFRICA OPERATION.

MADEMOISELLE CHANETTE WAS EDUCATED IN AG-RONOMICS IN MOSCOW, AND IS KNOWN TO HAVE BEEN RE-

CRUITED BY THE KGB DURING HER UNIVERSITY YEARS. (PHOTO ENCLOSED—SEE NSA FILE BLB-1974333)

Carter pulled a paper clip from the top of the page, and a five-by-seven photo of a woman dressed in a figure-fitting one-piece swimsuit fell into his hand. She was closer to thirty than twenty, with long, shining sable hair, striking green eyes, and a perfectly shaped and robust body.

Carter flipped the picture over. On the back was written SKOLNOV, BLACK SEA and the date the photograph was taken.

He went back to the Alvarez report.

CONTACT MADE WITH INSIDE MAN, A FISHERMAN, JORGE SILVA. FOR A PRICE (SEE ATTACHED FUNDING), SILVA HAS AGREED TO COOPERATE.

That was it.

Carter closed the folder and looked up. David Hawk stood, legs wide apart, cigar in one hand, drink in the other, staring moodily down at him.

"There must be more, if this was given to us from the Pentagon," Carter said, dropping the folder on Hawk's desk and opening his cigarette case.

"There is. Normally a doper operation wouldn't be in our area. This one is."

"Because the KGB is overseeing the growing and shipping?"

"That, and who it's being shipped to."

Hawk slid the mangled end of his cigar between his teeth, deftly picked a sheet of computer printout from the mountain of paper on the desk, and handed it to Carter.

Carter looked once, whistled, and then looked closer. "Jesus."

The sheet contained figures on the number of known and estimated heroin addicts among NATO personnel in Europe.

"You'll notice," Hawk growled, "that in the last year, since this operation started up in the Algarve, addiction has almost doubled."

Carter nodded. "A nice quiet way to undermine the troops. How's the stuff getting out of Portugal?"

"Don't know. But it looks like Commander Alvarez was getting close."

"And . . .?"

"And that's the last report we got from him. You'll notice it was dated two weeks ago."

"Yeah?"

"Alvarez disappeared the day after that report reached Brussels. He was a good man, well trained. He was of Spanish extraction but spoke fluent Portuguese. He made a mistake, obviously. What it was, we don't know."

"Any word?" Carter asked, drawing deeply on his cigarette.

"Day before yesterday, we heard from this contact he made, Jorge Silva. It came through his sister, an entertainer in Lisbon named Leonita Silva."

"And . . ."

"Alvarez is dead . . . murdered. Silva skipped the Algarve. He's in hiding now somewhere in the north . . . maybe Lisbon. He wants to make a deal; all he knows for fifty thousand American—in cash. You're set to make contact with the Silva woman tomorrow night. Bateman has your tickets, the fifty thou, and the contact info. Good luck, Nick."

That was all there was to it. Carter stood, shook hands with Hawk, and headed for the door. He knew he would get all the rest of it from Ginger Bateman. It was a good guess that she knew as much or more about the operation than did Hawk.

"Nick . . .?"

"Yes, sir?"

"Stay up-to-date daily . . . hourly, if things start to move."

"Of course."

"And, Nick . . ."

"Yes?"

"This Coco Chanette might be the North African half of the operation. Chances are we can't touch her. We want the Portuguese half. That's the biggie. When you find out that half, I'll let you know on any executive action."

"Yes, sir," Carter replied tight-lipped, then moved into Ginger Bateman's domain in the outer office.

"Executive action" was a polite euphemism for blowing somebody away.

Ginger Bateman was all business, ready and waiting for him.

"Here's a file on Maria "Coco" Chanette and Jorge Silva. Devour and burn 'em."

"Will do."

She draped a thick money belt over his arm. "Here's fifty thousand in hundreds and fifties. Sign for it."

"Gonna ruin my figure." Carter signed.

"Make sure it doesn't ruin anything else."

Carter rolled his eyes up. "My God, she smiles."

The smile quickly disappeared. "Your contact is one Miguel Avila, heat of Portuguese internal security. He's a good man, perhaps a little too much pride, but I don't think he'll get in your hair."

"Does he know about me?"

"No. As far as he knows, you're just another errand boy for NATO, a good snoop but not much else."

In the minutest detail, Ginger gave him the info on time, place, and intro for the meet with the sister, Leonita Silva.

"Is that it?"

"That's it. Good luck."

"Ginger . . ."

"Yes?"

"Care to walk to the elevator?"

Doubt creased her forehead, and for the briefest of

seconds her eyes clouded over. But she moved around the desk and into the hall beside him.

"Remember the Algarve?"

"Yes," she replied, keeping her eyes on the digital figures above the door.

Months before, after an assignment, Ginger had taken some time off, as had Carter. They had met in the Algarve and spent every moment together in a rented villa. It had been the culmination of vibrations that had been flowing between them for years.

"No involvement," she had said then. "Now is now, and tomorrow is then."

But Carter hadn't forgotten, and, now, he was glad she hadn't either.

"It was one hell of a vacation."

"Yes, it was."

She turned toward him of her own volition, and Carter tipped her chin up with one finger. When their lips met, they could both feel the shudder clear to their toes.

But, as if by mutual agreement, a foot of space was kept between their bodies.

"Be cool," she said, breaking the kiss at last and taking a step backward.

"Always."

"And come back."

"Always."

Her heels clicked a few steps down the hall, and then she paused and turned.

"Remember me to the Algarve."

"I will."

She disappeared around a corner, and Carter stepped into the elevator. As he reached up to push the lobby button, his elbow brushed against the hard steel of Wilhelmina under his arm.

That was all it took.

Emotions were okay, but they always had to take second place to survival.

TWO

Keeping one eye darting over his shoulder and both ears peeled for any sounds of following feet, Carter left the O Bistro. He took his bearings off the waters of the bay and headed toward the newer part of the city.

Getting out of the Alfama proved a great deal easier than getting in. Since the entire quarter was built against the side of a mountain, all he had to do was keep going down. Eventually he would hit one of the main boulevards that ran into the center of the new town.

The alleylike street was widening out and he could see the blue incandescence from the boulevard lights, when he caught the click of heels behind him.

Fifty yards farther on, he stopped. The other feet continued a few steps and then also stopped. Carter took a quick recon behind him. The street was empty, but then there were a hundred doorways someone could have popped into.

Carter retraced the fifty yards, rolling his eyes from side to side. He kept his forehead curled in concentration, as if he were lost and trying to find an address.

He had just passed a doorway near the top of the rise when a minuscule flash of white caught his eye in its dark depths. He turned at the first side street, then began running in place and from side to side. He also changed the sound by alternating from the heels of his boots to his soles to simulate distance.

Almost instantly the sound of pursuit came to his ears. When it was loud enough, Carter stopped running and flattened himself against a tiled wall.

His timing couldn't have been better. In fact, it was perfect. His shoulder blades had barely found the wall when the little man from O Bistro whirled around the corner, his eyes frantically searching the night.

Carter curled the fingers of his left hand around the man's tie and got his right shoulder against his narrow chest. As he yanked down with his left hand, Carter lifted and shoved with his shoulder, slamming the man's body against the wall.

There was a cry of pain, quickly followed by a gasping exhalation of air. Carter backed off, fully intending on slamming him clear through the wall on the second try, when the man managed to rasp out a few words.

"Enough . . . enough . . . *por favor*!"

Carter paused. He wound the tie tight with his left hand and moved his right down to the other's crotch. When he had a solid handful, Carter pushed his face close until the tip of his nose touched the other man's.

"I hope you've already got kids, you bastard, 'cause if you ain't got the right answers, you're never gonna have another one," he spat in English, hoping his captive understood his tone if not the words.

"Hey, man . . . easy! Take it easy!" he gasped in English, squirming and sweating as Carter's grip tightened. "Wallet . . . inside pocket, right side."

"Pull it out, slow, then flip it to the center of the street."

He did.

Carter released him but did a quick frisk as he pulled his hands away. They didn't leave empty. From a belt holster in the middle of the man's back, Carter withdrew a snub-nosed Walther PPK.

"They got strict laws against these toys in Portugal, pal."

"Check the wallet," the little man said, massaging the raw welt Carter had left on his neck.

Carter did, snapping the Walther's safety to "off" and keeping the muzzle on the man's belly.

"Pepe Laginha, Lieutenant, Portuguese Internal Security, Division One, Lisbon. This you?"

"Hell, yes. Picture's on the other side."

Carter flipped the plastic folder over in the wallet and held it up beside the man's face.

They matched.

"What's the beef with me?"

"No beef, man. I'm on Avila's staff. I'm supposed to follow you to make sure no one else does. Easy as that."

Carter handed over the wallet. "Your English is pretty American."

"Went to university in the States, Columbia School of Law. Jesus, you play rough. Can I have my gun back?"

"In a minute. Who am I?"

"Nick Carter, NATO special services . . . arrived Lisbon 6:47 this morning, TWA. Reason, the Algarve connection."

"What color is the carpet in Miguel Avila's office?"

"Jesus . . ."

"What color?" Carter barked.

"Puke green with a funny gold border."

Carter snapped the safety on the Walther, flipped it in his hand, and gave it back to Pepe Laginha.

"Thanks . . . I was just following orders."

"Wonderful," Carter growled. "Follow these . . . tell Avila I'm a nonperson. I'm not even here. So I don't need a watchdog."

"Hey, man, Lisbon can be rough at night."

"So can I."

Carter turned on his heel and headed back down the hill.

● ● ●

By the time Carter turned the little Seat through the huge stone pillars marking the winding drive up to the Castelo de São Jorge, the rain was coming down in earnest. Even on high, the wipers had a tough time keeping the windshield clear.

Three-quarters of the way to the top he swerved into a truck pull-out and stopped. Pulling the high collar of his trench coat around his head, he made the rest of the way on foot. He was just moving into a large courtyard above the castle's old outer wall, when the timer activated the cathedral chime sounding the half hour.

It was 3:30.

One light illuminated the wall below him. At one time, a couple of hundred years earlier, that area would have been lit all night by fires. The firelight would have been dancing off Moorish armor, and the snores of sleeping men and snorting horses would have filled the night air.

Now a single, low-wattage lamp cast faint shadows over ancient olive trees and well-manicured flower beds.

In the dim light Carter checked Wilhelmina's loads, rammed the magazine back home, and levered a shell into the chamber. He left the safety off and slid his gun hand into the right pocket of his coat as he moved down the narrow stone steps.

He was halfway across the ramparts when he spotted the cannons, six of them, arranged on both sides of a corner jutting toward the bay.

By the time he reached the cannons, instinct had taken over. Little ripples ran up and down the skin over his spine. It came from years of being in dark places and knowing you weren't alone.

"Nick . . ."

He knew immediately that it was her, the voice was so distinctive. She was far to his right, in the shadows of a huge, gnarled olive tree.

"Yes," he said, keeping his eyes toward the bay.

"You came alone?"

"Of course."

"You were followed from the club," she said.

"I know. His name is Pepe Laginha. Internal security. He's probably still somewhere behind me, but too far to make any difference. I took twenty detours before coming up here."

"Good. Did you bring the money?"

"Yes. Where's Jorge?"

"About an hour from here. Go back to your car. Take the narrow road around the wall. Just around the bay side corner there is a door in the wall. I will meet you there, and don't turn on your lights."

"Is all this necessary?"

"Yes!" she snapped. "The people who have been following and watching me this past week have not been from the police."

Carter retraced his steps to the Seat and moved out. Without lights he missed the narrow, rutted lane that led around the castle's outer wall, and he had to back up.

He had barely stopped in front of a dark indentation in the wall he assumed was the door, when she appeared.

"Follow this road around until it moves away from the wall. At the bottom, turn right. I'll tell you when to stop."

"Stop? I thought you said Jorge—"

"I did. We are going to my house first."

Carter shrugged and concentrated on his driving in the rain and almost pitch-black darkness.

"Stop here!"

"Is this your house?"

"No . . . there."

Carter followed her finger to a red-roofed, gaudily tiled two-story house two blocks away at the foot of a hill.

"You see, there, beyond my house under those trees?"

Carter leaned forward, squinting his eyes to see through the rain. "Yeah, I see . . . . a Mercedes, two men in the front seat."

"*Sim*. Now we wait."

It wasn't long, ten minutes to be exact, when a taxi pulled up in front of Leonita Silva's door. Within a minute a woman emerged and darted through the rain toward the taxi's open door.

It took a beat or two before Carter got the picture. The woman was dressed in knee-high gray boots, a red and gold full skirt that swirled as she ran, and a white blouse with large, puffed sleeves. Over her head, most of her face, and her shoulders was the traditional black shawl.

Beside him, Leonita Silva was dressed exactly the same way.

"Who is she?"

"My maid. Now we see."

The words had barely left her mouth when the taxi's taillights disappeared around a corner. In the distance, Carter heard the Mercedes's powerful engine roar into life. Then, lights off, it too rolled down the hill and around the same corner.

"You believe me now, Senhor Nick?"

"I believe you."

"Good. We go now . . . the other way."

"Where do we go?" Carter asked.

"You know Sintra?"

"*Sim.*"

"Good, we go to Sintra."

As Carter engaged the Seat's gearbox, he fully realized that the Silvas, Jorge and Leonita, had every reason to take precautions.

It looked as if both sides were playing for all the marbles.

Sintra lay north of Lisbon, beyond posh Estoril with its monstrous villas belonging to royalty and those who only pretended to the blood. The village was slightly inland from the sea, reached by a miniature version of Italy's treacherous Amalfi Drive.

Ridges of hibiscus, tamarisk, and colorful bougainvillea gave way to thick forests and rugged cliffs when the road left the sea. Here the hairpin turns, lack of shoulders, sheer cliffs, and five-hundred-foot drop-offs would put stark terror into the heart of any but the most callous Grand Prix driver.

Carter reveled in it. He throttled, braked, screamed around turns, donkey-drawn carts, Vespas, and early-morning, sleepy-eyed drivers like a pro.

Beside him, Leonita Silva took it all with Portuguese calm and acceptance of the inevitable. Once, when he had negotiated a particularly dangerous S-curve and come out the other side many revs up from when he had gone in, she even laughed.

"I think, Senhor Nick, you have a little Portuguese in your soul!"

"Oh? How so?"

"You enjoy the nearness of death, and you have no fear of danger."

"You see that in my driving?"

"Yes, and in your eyes . . . they are empty."

It was the only time she spoke until they flew over a final crest and found themselves among the ancient spires, battlements, and citadels of Sintra.

"Sintra," she said, a note of reverence in her voice. "*Sim.*"

Dawn was just breaking, bathing the pastel houses and shops in a warm glow. Once through the main square of the village, dominated by the huge conical twin chimneys of the National Palace, Leonita again started giving directions.

"Turn in there . . . the Hotel de Paraíso."

"A hotel?"

"*Sim.*"

No other explanation was offered, so Carter shrugged and turned in. It was a narrow, uphill lane, more like a one-way channel between ivy-covered stone walls several feet high. Above them, the morning sun was blotted out by giant oak and eucalyptus trees.

Suddenly they burst from the cover of the trees into a

small courtyard in front of a small Moorish-looking inn.

Carter braked before a set of winding stone steps, and Leonita slipped from the car.

"Wait here. I will get us a cottage."

Before Carter could object, she was gone. He lit a cigarette and almost at once extinguished it. The raspy smoke clawed at his lungs and burned his eyes, telling him that he had slept less than four hours in the last thirty-six.

"We have bungalow twelve . . . that way."

Until he heard the car door slam and her voice, Carter didn't realize that his eyes had closed and that he had very nearly drifted off to dreamland.

Careful, old man, he thought as he started the car. *Careless people soon get the* big *sleep!*

"Why the bungalow?" he asked, following Leonita inside.

"For you," she replied, "to sleep. I will contact Jorge this afternoon. We will meet him tonight."

She must have seen the weary thank-you in Carter's eyes, because her full, sensual lips curved in the semblance of a smile and she took his hand.

"This way."

She led him through a rustic living room, down a tiled hall, and into a well-appointed bedroom.

"You sleep, Senhor Nick. I will awaken you when I return."

Gratefully, Carter stripped out of his pea jacket and shirt. While she drew full-length drapes across a wall of windows, he pulled off his boots. She turned just as his fingers found the buckle of the thick money belt around his waist.

Their eyes met, and no words were needed by either of them to express their thoughts.

"We Portuguese are a very poor people," she said at last, "but we are also honest."

Carter removed the money belt and thoughtfully hefted it in his hand before answering her.

"Your brother, Jorge . . ."

"*Sim?*"

"Is *he* as honest as he is poor?"

The black coals of her eyes burned intensely for a few seconds, and then, as if on a switch, they dulled and misted over.

As she moved from the room in silence, Carter swore that she had aged ten years.

It wasn't a sound but a presence that lifted Carter abruptly from a deep sleep. Even before his eyes opened, his hand had found Wilhelmina beneath the pillow.

The drapes had been pulled open, but the room was dark. She sat, like a black-clad madonna, on the veranda. He could smell smoke from a harsh Moroccan cigarette and see the tendrils of gray lifting to float above her head.

Without turning, she spoke. "You are awake. Good. We eat, and then meet Jorge."

A quick shower made him half-whole again, and the fish, rice, and eggs she had ordered from the inn's kitchen did the rest.

In the car he was relieved to see that his hands were as steady on the wheel as if they were inanimate.

Amazing, he thought, what a little sleep would do.

"How far?"

"Ten minutes, driving," Leonita replied in a low voice, "then we walk."

While she concentrated on the road, Carter studied her out of the corner of his eye. The strong features and olive-toned skin of her face were oddly mysterious in the amber glow of the dashboard lights. Her nose, unlike most of her countrymen, was almost patrician, and her eyes never seemed to blink.

"You stare," she said, again without turning, as if she had eyes all around her head or could sense what she didn't see.

"Yes, I was. You are very beautiful."

"My mother was Moroccan," she said matter-of-factly. "Moroccans are very beautiful people. Stop there, beneath those trees."

Carter braked and eased the Seat in under the swaying limbs of a huge oak. He killed the lights and, in tandem with her, got out of the car.

"Where to now?"

"Up there," she said, pointing through the trees. "It is an abandoned house . . . a peasant who could not pay his rent."

It was nearly a mile through heavy undergrowth, trees, and over rocks taller than they were.

"How did you get here this afternoon?" Carter asked, feeling the strain of the climb in his legs.

"Walked," Leonita replied in a tight voice. "As a young girl I walked thirty kilometers every day to work in a Dutchman's house as a maid. I am used to walking."

The "house" was no more than a one-room stucco box with a low rock wall surrounding it. Burlap covered holes where there had never been windowpanes, and a sheet of tin served as a door.

When they reached a gate that was held in place by only one hinge, Leonita stopped Carter with a hand on his elbow.

"Jorge?" she called.

"*Sim,*" came a guttural reply from the darkened depths of the hut.

Brother and sister spoke briefly in Portuguese, but Carter had trouble getting the gist of their conversation.

"What did he say?" he growled, frustrated.

"He asks if you are armed. I told him yes."

"Does he speak English?"

"Yes, I do, *senhor*. Give your gun to my sister."

Carter lifted Wilhelmina from her holster under the pea jacket and held it up so Jorge could see. Then he levered the magazine into his hand and handed it to Leonita.

"This will keep us both honest," he said, managing a smile. "All right, Silva, what now?"

"Come in. Leonita . . . keep watch on the path."

"*Sim*," she nodded, then melted into the shadows.

Carter moved slowly up the path. There was no rain and only a light breeze, but he could feel a chill creeping up his spine. Instinctively he bunched the muscles of his right forearm to test the spring action in Hugo's chamois sheath.

The tin door was slightly ajar and tilting inward. Carter stepped through the opening, and his nostrils were immediately assaulted with the smell of manure and decaying straw.

"Jorge?"

"I am here. Have you matches?"

"A lighter," Carter replied.

"Good. Walk straight ahead . . . slowly. There is a table in front of you with two candles on it. Light them, *por favor*."

Carter did as he was told, then quickly cased the single room in the two tapers' dancing flames. Dirt floor littered with straw, a filthy cot, the table, and two rickety chairs. Atop the table, beside the candles, were two cracked cups and an opened bottle of wine.

"As you can see," Silva said, moving into the light across the table from Carter, "I've prepared for your visit. It isn't the best port, but it is all I could steal."

Jorge Silva was inches taller than Nick's six-two, and wafer thin. Unruly black hair hung to his shoulders and exploded all over his head in tight curls. A week's worth of stubble on his face didn't agree with the heavy black mustache that completely covered his upper lip.

Right now the mustache was quivering almost as much as the .45 automatic he held in his right hand.

Carter couldn't suppress a smile. Jorge Silva might be a small-time hoodlum and smuggler, but he sure didn't know much about guns. He was holding the .45 at his hip at an awkward angle, as if he'd gotten his shooting lessons from an old Grade B Hollywood Western.

"You find something amusing about the gun, *senhor?*"

"A little," Carter replied. "It's hard to fire a .45 with the top safety on."

Silva's eyes dropped instinctively, saw that the safety was off, and reacted by literally leaping backward two steps. At the same time, he brought the gun up with both hands until the muzzle was wavering between Carter's head and chest.

"Don't play with me," he cried. "You hear? Don't play with me!"

The last was almost shouted, and it brought a cry from Leonita outside.

"Jorge . . . Jorge, are you all right?"

"*Sim . . . sim*, get back to the road."

During the exchange, Carter took a closer look. Jorge Silva was younger than he had expected, probably in his very early twenties. But there was age in his wild eyes and in the weathered wrinkles around them. There was also fear in those eyes, the kind of fear that makes a man do crazy things for little or no reason.

"Calm down, Jorge, I'm on your side," Carter said. "If I had wanted to, I could have taken that gun away from you just now."

"Not before I put a bullet in your belly!"

Carter shrugged. Slowly he pulled the shirt from his pants. When the money belt was exposed, he unbuckled it and laid it across the table.

"The money?" Silva asked, his eyes like devouring black claws.

"Yes."

Carter poured wine into both cups. He offered the one in his right hand to Silva. "Friends?" he said.

The gun lowered slightly as Silva reached warily for the cup. Just as his fingertips touched the cup, Carter released it. At the same time, he tensed the muscles in his right forearm, sending the pencil-thin stiletto, Hugo, into his hand.

The other man's natural reaction was to grab for the cup, which he did, only to find an eighth of an inch of steel in his throat just below his jaw.

"I'll bet you the fifty thousand on that table, son, that I can put the point of this stiletto in your brain before you can put a bullet in my gut."

"Don't . . . don't do it!" Silva gurgled, the fear in his eyes coming out now in beads of sweat on his face.

"Then put that gun on the table before I take it away from you and shove it up your ass."

With another gurgled cry that sounded more like a whine, Silva inched forward and to the side until he could place the automatic on the table.

"I . . . I didn't mean anything. I'm scared, that's all . . . very scared. Paragem wants me dead. They killed your man, they'll kill me . . . he said he'd take care of me . . ."

"Slow down, for Christ's sake, and relax," Carter said, jabbing the point of the stiletto into the tabletop and jacking the magazine out of the .45.

Jorge Silva sat down on one of the chairs, and tears were streaming from his eyes. He held his hands between tightly-pressed knees to keep them from shaking. It didn't help. His whole body was shaking.

You, Carter thought, *are not made of the same stuff as your sister.*

He retrieved the now empty cup from the floor and refilled it.

"Here, this may calm you down. Now let's talk. Who's Paragem?"

THREE

Until a year and a half before, José Paragem had been merely a fish broker along the Algarve. He worked from Faro all the way west to Sagres. But his office and most of his dealings were done in and around the harbor town of Portimão.

About that time, Paragem had started contacting fishermen known to be on the shady side of the law and in trouble keeping up the payments on their boats.

They weren't hard to find.

Competition for the fish all across the Algarve and up the western coast of Portugal was keen. Thousands of single fishermen and entire families went out daily. Many of them came back dry.

It was only natural that a few of them went more than just a mile or two offshore to secure a night's catch that didn't have scales or fins. Everything from hashish to gems to illegal ivory could be loaded in the inlets around Tangier, Morocco, and sold for high profit in Lisbon.

For many, smuggling under the guise of fishing became a way of life.

These were the men José Paragem sought out, and Jorge Silva was one of them.

Legally, Paragem would buy both fisherman and boat. This did away with the need to conform to the "open bid"

29

law whereby each catch, upon hitting port, had to be put up for bid by all the brokers. By leasing the boat at a flat rate, Paragem already owned the catch.

"We would be sent out, ten or twelve of us, three times a week on staggered nights. We never knew until we were at sea, often with our nets already out, if that was to be the night."

"And if it was?" Carter asked, drawing deeply on his cigarette.

"We monitored a certain frequency each time for weather reports and commercial fishing tips. If a tip came over that 'the shrimp are running off Sagres,' we knew that we were to rendezvous with a freighter after she had cleared the Gibraltar strait."

"These freighters . . . do you remember their names or ports of call?"

"No," Silva replied, nervously fingering the cup of wine in his hands, "but they were always Algerian or Libyan."

"Go on."

"We would rendezvous at sea at fifteen-minute intervals. Each boat would take on two crates, unmarked."

"All ten of them?"

Silva nodded. "But only one boat would be carrying the hard stuff. None of us ever knew which of us it was."

"And then?"

"Each of us had a drop-off point for our night's catch. It was given to us in a sealed envelope before leaving Portimão at dusk."

"Ten boats," Carter mused, "coming in at ten different places on the Algarve."

"Exactly. Very hard, almost impossible, to pinpoint."

"And where did the crates go once they were ashore?"

"Always they were full of dry ice. Right at the beach, the catch would be sorted and stored. Then the crates were loaded on trucks and taken away. I did learn from a loose-lipped truckdriver that some of the crates were delivered right to the kitchens of the large hotels. Others were sent to Faro for export.''

Carter mashed his cigarette out and immediately lit another. Obviously the crates that went to Faro contained the fish—and the heroin—that eventually found its way to NATO bases.

"This Paragem, Jorge . . . what kind of man is he?"

Silva shrugged. "A businessman, *senhor*. He deals in profit.''

"Does he have what it takes to set up an operation like this?"

"I don't know. Your man, Alvarez, didn't think so. He was sure that José Paragem was only . . . what you call . . .''

"A front?"

"*Sim*, a front. He hired the fishermen, the boats, and got the merchandise moved. Someone else, a more powerful man, took over from there.''

"Tell me about Alvarez . . . and you.''

Silva's dark face paled visibly. Once again his hands started shaking, and suddenly his eyes began darting around the room.

"Alvarez came to my house one night. He showed me photographs. They were taken at night in a cove near Vilamoura . . .''

"Of you unloading the crates from your boat.''

"*Sim*. How do photos get taken at night, and from such a distance?"

"With a telephoto lens and a camera rigged with infrared. Never mind . . . go on.''

"He told me that he had other proof that I and my countrymen were smuggling raw opium. He knew about my police record. He said that if I did not help him he would expose me.''

Carter felt a tug in his gut as he watched the other man's shifty eyes search out every corner of the hut as if he could find a hiding place to crawl in, away from Carter's penetrating stare. Silva's face was almost like a graph on a lie detector machine; each time he came close to a lie, more sweat popped from its pores.

"Ramon Alvarez also offered to pay you for your help, didn't he, Jorge?"

"A little."

"About fifty thousand dollars cash, Jorge?"

"Yes," he whined. "And I earned it! I broke the seal on a crate to find out what it contained. I drank with the drivers to find out where the crates went. I slept with a servant girl in Paragem's house to find out who visited him. I earned the money!"

"All right," Carter sighed. "How did Ramon Alvarez get it?"

The amount of sweat rolling into Silva's eyes doubled. Cursing, he ground his thumbs over the lids to clear them.

"He wanted to make a run with me. He said he had found out the African source of the opium and was pretty sure he knew the name of Paragem's boss. He wanted a look himself inside one of the crates. I told him he was crazy, but he insisted."

"And what did he find in the crates?"

"Sometimes rock salt instead of dry ice."

Carter digested this for a minute or two, then popped the question that had been nagging at him since the conversation had begun.

"Who killed Ramon Alvarez?"

"I don't know."

"Jorge." Carter didn't attempt to hide the ominous tone he let creep into his voice. It brought out more sweat on Silva's brow.

"I mean I don't know his name . . . even what he looks like. The night Alvarez went with me on the run, we returned our catch and the crates to a cove near Carvoeiro . . ."

"That's the beach village just south of Lagoa?"

"*Sim*. I had explained to Paragem that I had taken on

another hand for the night because my regular mate, a young boy, was sick. I said Alvarez was a lover of my sister and could be trusted.''

"And Paragem bought it?''

"I though so . . . then. But when we hit the cove that night, there was no truck to meet us, only a sedan with a woman and two men. One of the men was Paragem's driver. The woman was tall, very beautiful, with dark hair. The second man was dressed in a heavy knit cap like yours. He also wore a coat with a high collar, and he stayed in the shadows near the rocks . . .''

"Well?'' Carter asked after a long pause.

"I'm trying to remember it exactly as it happened.''

"Are you, Jorge . . . or are you making it up as you go along?''

"No, damn you, I . . . when we jumped from the boat to the beach, the woman and the driver covered us with automatic rifles. The driver kept me near the boat while the woman marched Alvarez to the rocks where the other man waited.''

Here Silva paused again. He drained the wine from his cup and refilled it before continuing.

"They talked—Alvarez, the man, and the woman—for a long time. Then Alvarez started back toward the driver and me, followed by the other two. They were about halfway across the beach when the woman started firing, hitting Alvarez in the back. She . . . just . . . kept . . . shooting. By the time she stopped she had almost cut the poor bastard in half!''

"And what did you do?'' Carter asked, watching the sweat drip from the other man's quivering chin.

"Do? You crazy? What could I do? I pissed my pants. The woman told me to stuff the body into one of the crates and then dump everything—catch and all—as far out to sea as I could get before dawn.''

"Odd, Jorge. Why didn't they waste you?''

"Waste?''

"Shoot you . . . kill you."

Silva shrugged. He also tried to meet Carter's eyes with his own, but still couldn't.

"The only thing I could think of was what else she said. She told me Alvarez was a plant from the police. She said that from then on I'd better watch who I used on the boat and that they would be watching me."

Carter sighed and stood. He lifted the money belt from the table and started winding it around his middle.

"Hey, what are you doing?"

"Keeping the fifty thousand," Carter replied calmly. "Your story stinks, Silva. You lie like a snake."

His hand was quick, darting toward the stiletto stuck in the table, but Carter's was quicker. He caught Silva's hand and forearm, lifted, and then brought the wrist down over the edge of the table.

The sharp crack of the breaking bone was quickly followed by the man's scream of pain.

"You're lucky that's all I break," Carter hissed, his face bare inches from Silva's. "The only reason I don't kill you is because of your sister. She thinks you're human."

"Jesus, you broke it! You broke my arm!"

The door burst open and Leonita Silva charged a few steps into the room. As usual her face was a mask, hiding any emotion she felt, even after seeing the situation.

"What is it? What happened?" she asked calmly.

"I broke his wrist," Carter replied evenly. "The deal was information for money. He's been lying to me ever since I stepped into the room."

"Does he speak the truth, Jorge?"

"*Não!* I swear it!"

"Crap," Carter said. "We've got a running file on you—both before and after Alvarez's death. We knew every move you made until you skipped the Algarve. Alvarez never got you paid because he got clipped before he could do it. But two days before he bought it, you laundered fifty thousand through a Eurobond merchant in Tangier.''

''Is that true, Jorge?'' Leonita gasped. Her face, for the first time since Carter had met her, showed a little emotion as she took a couple of steps toward her brother. ''You told me you were broke, that you needed this American money to get out of Portugal and stay alive.''

''It is true, Leonita, I swear it!''

''More crap, Jorge,'' Carter said. ''My guess is you turned Alvarez in to Paragem, or to the big man himself, collected from him, and then took off when you saw the results. Murder, you hadn't counted on. When you actually saw it happen, you figured you just might be next. You're a rat, Jorge, and a greedy one. You figured you'd collect from us as well.''

Silva sat cringing in the chair, holding his left wrist with his right hand.

Leonita leaned close to her brother. ''Does this man speak the truth, Jorge? Have you been lying to him after agreeing to take his money?''

Silva didn't answer, but through the contorted mask of pain on his face, both Carter and Leonita saw the truth.

Suddenly the woman came alive. She was on her brother like a cat with its claws bared. She hit him, and kept hitting him with her palm and the back of her hand on the backswing. Jorge's head snapped back and forth like a metronome on his shoulders while he begged her to stop and to forgive him.

And with every blow came an angry, machine-gun patter full of venom from Leonita's lips.

It was impossible for Carter to understand all the furious Portuguese spewing in long, livid phrases from her lips, but he caught some, such as, ''. . . coward . . . jackal . . . cringing, lying dog . . .'' and so on.

He also got the general impression that Jorge had been the bad seed in the Silva family since birth. It was his shame that had driven their mother to an early grave, and his wasted life that had put all the lines of worry on Leonita's face.

Suddenly she stopped, panting, her face dripping perspiration, her ample breasts heaving in the thin blouse.

"He will tell you what you wish to know, Senhor Nick," she said, stepping aside.

Even though blood and violence were everyday aspects of Carter's life, he winced slightly when he saw Jorge Silva's face.

It was hamburger: raw, blood-dripping meat.

Evidently Leonita had curled her fingers into claws every other stroke. In so doing, her long crimson nails had made a mess of her brother's features.

"What really happened that night?" Carter whispered.

"I didn't betray Alvarez. They knew all along who he was."

"But you set him up?"

"Yes. That night we didn't pick up any crates from the freighter. We picked up the woman."

Carter fished the swimsuit photo of Coco Chanette from an inside pocket. "Was this the woman?"

"Yes."

Carter replaced the photo. "Go on."

"While I manned the rudder, they talked. I only heard part of it, but . . . enough."

Here he paused, and then he darted his eyes toward his sister. He spoke to her so fast, in such clipped sentences, that Carter was sure he couldn't have caught it even if his Portuguese were excellent.

"Hold it! What's he saying, Leonita?"

"He says you will never believe him."

"Let me be the judge of that. Spill it, Jorge!"

"Alvarez explained to the woman that he was not connected with the Portuguese authorities. He was with NATO, on special assignment from . . . sharp . . .?"

"SHAPE. Why was he getting so chummy with the woman?"

Again Silva turned pleading eyes on his sister. Her only answer was to raise her hand.

"I'll tell him, I'll tell him! Alvarez told her he knew the whole operation. He wanted in. He said that by filing false progress reports he could stall any more agents for at least a year."

Carter's face turned grim. Now it was his turn to step forward and menace Jorge. He yanked the young man to his feet by his jacket lapels and pulled him forward until their noses almost touched.

"You'd better not be lying about this. Alvarez had a good military record, and he had a wife and two kids in the States."

"I'm not! This time I swear I'm not!"

This time Carter believed him. He released the hold on his jacket, and Silva slumped back in the chair like a rag doll.

"He told the woman that in the States he was a 'spic,' and Hispanics don't get to be admirals. He wanted money . . . lots of it."

"How much did you hear about the operation?"

"Damn little . . . it's the truth. But Alvarez did scare her when he told her who the head of the Algarve connection was."

"Who?" Carter said, louder than he had intended.

"I didn't hear the name, but I did hear Alvarez say that he and the man went way back. I don't know what that means."

"It means that they knew each other a long time."

"*Sim* . . . I think in Washington."

"Are you sure of that? In Washington?"

"*Sim,*" Silva nodded, "I am sure. He said it several times."

"Then what happened?"

Jorge chewed his lip until Carter thought he was going to burst into tears. "She shot him. I was turned away from them when she fired the first shot. I turned and watched her shoot him again. She just kept shooting until the gun was empty and his blood was everywhere. I did not lie when I told you she nearly cut him in half.''

"And then . . .?''

"She reloaded the pistol and turned to face me. God help me, she was smiling! She commanded me to help her weight him down. I did, and we dumped him to the fishes, there in the ocean. Then she told me to take her to the cove I mentioned, just east of the village of Carvoeiro. I . . . I . . .''

"All of it, Jorge,'' Leonita snapped.

"I steered toward the cove and purposely missed a buoy. When the bow hit a sandbar and the boat heeled over, I jumped. She fired at me several times but missed in the darkness.''

"So then you got the bright idea of coming to Lisbon and having your sister contact us.''

"*Sim*,'' he said, dropping his chin to his chest.

"*Jesus Cristo!*'' Leonita spat. "How much lower must you sink in this life before the devil claims you in the next?''

Carter unfastened the buckle of the money belt and draped it across the table. "There's your blood money, Silva. I hope that, and what you've already got stashed, will get you far enough away, but I doubt it.''

"*Obrigado*,'' came the mumbled reply of thanks.

"No!''

Deftly Leonita speared the money belt from the table and held it aloft.

"Leonita,'' Jorge hissed, his eyes suddenly gone wild and mad through the blood that had caked around them. "Enough from you, a woman, for this day!''

"*Não!*'' she said, glaring back at him in defiance. "It is blood money, and your hands are bloody enough, my brother. Don't soil your soul and make it any blacker! Here, Senhor Nick, take the money and leave us!''

She thrust the belt toward Carter, but before it reached

his hands Jorge had leaped from the chair. He snatched the belt from his sister's grasp and sent her sprawling with a shove from his shoulder at the same time.

Carter braced himself for the same kind of push from his other shoulder, but it never came. Instead, Jorge hit the table with his butt and rolled over it. He landed on his feet, and before Carter could grab him he was out the door.

"Jorge!" Leonita cried, gaining her own feet and lunging after her brother.

"Let him go, Leonita," Carter said. "You're better off."

She had one foot through the opening between the makeshift tin door and the stucco jamb, when the night outside the house exploded in gunfire.

There were two sharp cracks from a rifle, one right on top of the other.

Leonita froze in mid-step, her head swiveling until her eyes caught Carter's.

"Get back," he hissed, then lurched to one of the windows.

Cautiously he curled back a corner of the burlap and peered over the edge.

Jorge lay on the very edge of the trees about twenty yards from the house. The money belt was across his chest, and his head was spread all over the ground nearby.

"What is it? Is Jorge . . .?"

She was at his shoulder, her hands like a vise around his bicep.

"Yes. He's dead, Leonita . . . and in not a very pretty way."

If Carter expected wailing and hysterics, he got none. She released the hold on his arm, took a step backward, and quickly crossed herself. A few mumbled words that sounded like a prayer formed on her lips, and then she raised her head to stare at Carter. Her eyes were clear and dry.

"What are we to do?"

"Stay alive."

The words had barely left Carter's mouth when the rifle cracked again. There was a sickening thump near where his hand rested on the burlap, and both of them were showered with tiny flecks of stucco.

"Stay back!" Carter cried, shoving Leonita against the wall.

With his eyes and mind he did a quick perusal of the building's interior and an assessment of their situation.

There was little doubt that whoever the shooter was, he or they wanted Carter as well as Jorge, and, very likely, Leonita too.

No witnesses.

There were two burlap-covered windows and the door in front, nothing on the sides, and one opening in the rear wall. It was high up, and little more than a vent or air hole, but it looked big enough to wriggle through.

Moving in a crouch, Carter padded to the table. Quickly he extinguished the candles and discarded them. Groping, he found Hugo and Jorge's .45. He resheathed the stiletto and jammed the magazine back into the .45, levering a shell into the chamber in the same motion. Then he skidded the table across the dirt floor until it was just beneath the rear window.

He climbed on top of the table and cautiously wiggled the burlap.

Nothing.

"Well," he sighed in a throaty whisper, "here goes nothing . . . or everything."

He ripped away the burlap, and for a full three seconds exposed himself in the dim moonlight streaming through the opening.

Again, nothing.

Either there was only one of them, or a second shooter wasn't positioned to get a clear view of the rear wall.

Carter rolled off the table and moved back over the dirt floor to where Leonita stood, calmly watching his every move. Along the way he picked up one of the two chairs and mangled it until only a leg remained in his hand.

When he was near the window, he reached over and ruffled the burlap. The movement was answered immediately by a crack from the rifle and a shower of stucco chips.

"Give me my Luger," Carter said, turning to Leonita. "And take this!"

He passed her the .45, then reloaded Wilhelmina.

"This is the trigger, this is the muzzle. You squeeze this and point this, not necessarily in that order. Got it?"

"*Sim*," she said and nodded.

"I'm going out that little window and will try to flank them. When you see me disappear, start counting to thirty. When you get there, take the table leg and draw his fire. Do it again every minute or so from both windows. If you want to get real adventurous, stick the gun a little way out the door opening and give him a shot. Okay?"

She nodded again, and Carter smiled. She was as calm and cool as she had been hours before, standing in a spotlight, haughtily staring out at her audience.

"One more thing . . ."

"*Sim?*"

"If they try to rush that door before I can find them, get back there, against the wall, in a crouch. Hold the gun with both hands, like this."

"I understand."

"Aim for the gut, right in the middle, and keep firing until nothing moves. Got that?"

"They killed Jorge," she calmly replied. "It will be as nothing to kill them."

Carter knew she meant it.

The wires inside his body grew taut as he again exposed his upper body at the window and then heaved himself through. He lit on the mossy ground below like a cat, moving.

Forty yards into the woods, he started his flanking

movement. He ran in a zigzag pattern twenty yards at a
time, and then stopped to listen. Twice the rifle cracked
from the woods in front of the house, telling him that
Leonita was doing her job.

On the fifth such move, when he was about midway
around the wide semicircle that would take him to the
sniper's position, he heard the .45 answer the rifleman's
fire.

And then he heard something else: movement through
the trees about fifty yards in front of him.

So, Carter thought, *there* are *more than one of them*.

He slid his hand under the pea jacket, withdrew
Wilhelmina, and settled down behind a large oak to wait.

The wind was nil now, allowing him to hear every step
as the second shooter approached. When Carter was sure,
from the sound of cracking branches and rustling limbs,
that there was only one, he replaced Wilhelmina in his
right hand with Hugo.

The thin, boned hilt was barely nestled in his palm
when a short, barrel-chested man with a wide, flat face
that looked as if someone had stepped on it too many times
burst through a tangle of vines.

He was only three feet from the oak when Carter rolled
around it from the man's blind side. He came up, in an
underhand swing, with the stiletto. His intention was to
gut-stab the man and then chop his windpipe with his free
hand to choke off any cry.

He was a beat too late.

The man sidestepped Carter's thrust with alarming agil-
ity for one with such a short, compact body. At the same
time, he swung both hands as one, his clenched fists
catching Carter on the back of his right elbow. If Carter
hadn't followed through, high, on his swing, the blow
could have broken his arm.

As it was, Hugo slipped from Carter's grasp, and the
force of the blow spun him around twice before his back
slammed against a tree.

Like a gorilla—crouched, his arms low—the man came for Carter. Just before they came together, his right hand dived into his boot, coming up with a blade of his own.

But Carter was ready.

He bent low and came up under the gorilla's ponderously swung arm. At the same time, he brought his knee up with bone-crushing force into the man's crotch.

As the other's weight sagged against him, Carter slid Wilhelmina from her holster. Savagely he brought the butt of the Luger down across the man's neck. There was an animallike gasp of pain, and Carter struck again, this time missing the neck but making soft pulp out of a section in the back of his skull.

Slowly the man's knees bent. But even as he fell, his heavily muscled, corded arms wound around Carter's middle like the tentacles of an octopus.

Jesus, Carter thought, *the bastard isn't human!*

The pressure increased until Carter felt his intestines being squeezed up, like jelly, into his rib cage. Twice he pounded the top of the man's skull, all to no avail.

Then, when it seemed the very life was being squeezed from him, Carter levered the man's head away from his middle by forcing his chin up with his left hand. With all the force in his right arm, Carter brought the barrel of the Luger down in a smashing blow between the man's eyes.

The pressure on Carter's belly was immediately eased.

Carter stepped backward out of the deadly embrace and swung again.

It wasn't needed. The man was already dead, precariously balanced on his knees. Carter stepped to the side and nudged the body with his leg. It teetered for a second, then fell forward, like a timbered log.

Carter leaned against a tree for a few moments, massaging feeling back into his belly and regaining his breath. The air around him was still, the ground speckled with moonlight through the thick trees above.

The firing from the trees and the house had stopped.

Carter rolled the body over and tugged until light fell across the man's face. The skin was as dark as mahogany and the features blunt.

Portuguese?

Carter doubted it, and a quick search of his pockets proved it.

The passport looked authentic. The name was Alazar Kabib, and he was a citizen of Algeria . . . from Oran, to be exact.

Carter pocketed the passport, retrieved Hugo, and moved on. He skirted the trees until he could get a sighting from the windows of the house. When he was pretty sure of the sniper's angle of fire, he moved into the brush slowly, without a sound.

The sniper was only about twenty yards off to Carter's right. He was about forty feet up, balanced over a limb flat out on his belly.

Carter squatted with his back against a tree. He wrapped his left hand around his right wrist and rested both forearms on his raised knees.

It was a dead-out shot. Over half the man's body was illuminated against the moonlit sky. In contrast, Carter was buried in darkness.

If the gorilla had been Algerian, Carter assumed this one was as well. Consequently, he called out in French.

"Pardon, monsieur. Your compatriot Monsieur Kabib is very dead. If you do not wish to join him, I suggest you throw down your rifle."

Carter saw the man's head swivel around. He knew he couldn't be spotted, but he could imagine the man's eyes frantically searching the trees in the direction of Carter's voice.

"You have two seconds."

Carter caught the glint of moonlight on the rifle barrel as the man changed position and swung the gun into play.

"Damn fool," Carter hissed.

Without hurrying, he squeezed Wilhelmina's trigger. It was like hitting the broad side of a barn at twenty paces.

The Luger kicked, the body in the tree raised up, and then seemed to float out into space.

Carter was up and running before the sniper hit the ground.

He landed in a small clearing about ten feet from his rifle. When Carter crashed through the brush, the sniper was already crawling to retrieve his gun.

"Don't do it, my friend. I can hit you more easily from this distance than I did when you were playing monkey up there."

The crawling figure neither looked up nor halted his forward progress.

Carter raised the Luger and aimed.

"Last chance."

The groping figure found the rifle butt and began tugging it toward his other hand.

Carter fired.

The slug caught him dead center in the back of the neck. He twitched once, then lay still.

With his toe Carter rolled him over.

Guts, he thought. He had to give them both that.

Carter's first shot had caught the man in the belly. The pain had to be blinding, but not only had he not made a sound, he had gone out trying to get the rifle and take Carter with him.

A quick search of the man's pockets produced nothing. Of the two this one was the pro, Carter thought. The gorilla was probably just hired help.

He left the body where it had fallen and moved back toward the house. He stopped where Jorge Silva lay and stripped the body of all identification. Then he buckled the money belt back around his middle and headed for the house.

"Leonita . . .?"

"*Sim.*"

"Come on out, it's over."

He caught her just as she emerged from the house, blocking, with his own body, the sight of Jorge.

From the trembling of her lower lip and the mascara running down her cheeks, Carter realized that at last she had cracked. In a way he was glad.

Fear is an important aspect of survival; without it one can become reckless.

"There were two of them, hired guns. They're both dead."

She swayed forward and Carter caught her in one arm.

"*Obrigado*, Senhor Nick," she murmured, letting all her weight come to rest on his arm.

Then suddenly both her arms went around his neck, and she buried her face in his shoulder. Carter tensed slightly. He could feel the softness of her body against him and realized that she was shivering.

"Go back to the car," he whispered.

"What are you going to do?"

"There must be a shovel around here somewhere. I'm sorry, Leonita, but it's the only way."

"I understand," she murmured and walked around him.

She averted her eyes as she passed her brother, and as soon as she was out of sight, Carter went to work.

He was just throwing limbs and dead leaves over the fresh graves when she reappeared.

"Which one?"

Carter pointed, and he watched her slide to her knees at the head of the grave.

"I'll wait for you in the car," he said, already moving down the path.

Two cigarettes later she slid into the seat beside him.

"What will you do now?" she asked.

"The Algarve," he replied, mashing the cigarette in the dashboard ashtray.

"I will go with you."

Carter studied her carefully. "You're sure . . ."

"*Sim*. He was no good, but he was my brother. I will go with you."

FOUR

They drove along the coastal road back down to Lisbon in silence, each submerged in his own thoughts of recent events and what might await them beyond the capital city.

Carter went over every detail of Jorge Silva's story. He slot-filed it in the memory bank of his mind, which, over the years, he had trained to instant recall when the occasion arose.

Then he went over the file Bateman had given him on Maria "Coco" Chanette.

She had been born thirty-three years before, to an Algerian mother and a Marxist-loving French father.

From birth she had evidently been weaned on Communist ideology. She was not only a beautiful child, but quite gifted mentally. She had a scientific bent that her father had encouraged. When the time came for higher education, she was sent to a university in Moscow.

Ideally, her father had wanted her to study agronomics in the Soviet Union, then return to Algeria to teach. Somewhere along the line, however, that plan had been sidetracked by a KGB recruiter.

Chanette had indeed studied agriculture and its attendant subjects, but she had also gone through the Marx-Engels School for Political Indoctrination at Gorky. From there she had gone through the extensive KGB select training school in Moscow.

There had been no mention in Chanette's file as to whether she had completed the full course at the KGB school in both its categories: *chistaya rabota*—clean work—and *gryaznaya rabota*—dirty work.

If Jorge Silva's story was true about Chanette calmly wasting Ramon Alvarez, Carter was pretty sure Chanette was more highly trained than her Washington file would indicate.

The rest of her dossier had been a smattering of her accomplishments and travels.

Four years earlier, she had returned to Moscow for further schooling, this time in biology.

All in all, Coco Chanette was highly trained and highly educated. Too much so, Carter reasoned, to waste running a doper operation. Agents like her were rare. They were usually trained and groomed for one big operation, an operation much larger and more meaningful than growing and distributing heroin.

Unless there was more to the Algarve connection than just smuggling dope to hooked NATO troops.

Nick hit the outskirts of Lisbon and drove at once to the Lisboa Plaza. Leaving Leonita in the lobby, he retrieved his bag and checked out. There were two messages at the desk to contact Miguel Avila.

Carter made a scrambler phone call to Dupont Circle in Washington first.

Even with the time difference, Hawk was on the line seconds after the connection was made with Ginger Bateman.

Carter brought the head of AXE up-to-date on Jorge Silva, his version of the Algarve connection, and his demise.

When he finished, Killmaster N3 could almost hear the gears in his superior's mind whirring, sifting through Carter's report.

"What about the sister?" Hawk asked. "Could she be more than she appears?"

"She could be," Carter replied, "but I doubt it. In any event, she wants to make the Algarve with me, so I can keep an eye on her."

"You think that's wise?"

"No, but I've got a feeling I can't stop her, so I might as well have her around. She knows the people and the territory. She could be a lot of help."

"When do you head out?"

"In a couple of hours. I'm going to trade cars just in case we were spotted by someone else other than the two snipers I nailed."

"How much stock do you put in this story of Alvarez shifting gears on us?"

Hawk's voice, as he asked the question, had a lot of bite to it. It was never pleasant thinking of one of your own as a sell-out.

"I buy it," Carter growled. "By the time he spilled it, Silva didn't have a hell of a lot of reason to lie. Can you get someone right on it? Chances are whoever Alvarez knew in Washington who is now active in the Algarve was probably in the military."

"I'll put people on it within the hour—friends, co-workers, drinking buddies—the works."

"Good. Also check out the wife, for whatever it's worth."

"Will do. And, Nick . . ."

"Yes, sir?"

"It sounds a lot dirtier than we had figured. Use your own discretion on executive action."

"Will do."

Carter hung up, unscrewed the scrambler from the mouthpiece, and dialed a local number.

"I am sorry, Senhor Carter, but Inspector Avila is at lunch. Can you leave a message?"

"*Sim*. Tell him I called, and I will call back in one hour."

"*Obrigado. Adeus.*"

Carter grabbed his bag and reentered the lobby.

"Do you have a telephone at your place?"

"Of course," Leonita Silva replied.

"Good. Let's go. You can pack fast, I hope. I want to trade cars before we head south."

"Do you think . . .?" She paused, a hand resting lightly on his arm.

"Well?"

"Do you think it is safe, Senhor Nick, to return to my home?"

"I don't know," he replied. "But if someone is still on our back, we might as well know it now and flush him out. Oh, and do me a favor . . ."

"Sim?"

"Forget the *'senhor'* and just make it Nick, okay?"

"Okay," she replied, letting her lovely features break into a wide, warm smile.

It was the first real smile she had allowed herself since they had met. Carter liked it. It looked good on her.

This time they skirted the Alfama to make some speed. Ten minutes after leaving the Lisboa Plaza, Carter was parking the Seat on a narrow side street a block from Leonita's house.

"Key," he said, then slipped it into his pocket when she passed it over. "Do you have a watch?"

"Sim."

"Wait ten minutes and then follow me. If either one of us is going to draw some fire, it might as well be me. I get paid for it."

Carter stepped from the car and was about to move away when she spoke, stopping him.

"Senhor . . . uh, Nick . . ."

"Yes?"

"You are more than just a soldier or an international policeman, aren't you?"

"A little," he said, squeezing her hand where it rested on the car's open window. "Keep looking over your shoulder."

Both streets were clear. Only a few stray dogs roamed in the warm afternoon sun, and a group of boys were playing soccer in a vacant area between two houses near the corner.

Carter made the turn and moved toward the house. He listened for new sounds behind him and from every doorway he passed. His eyes flickered to scan windows and rooftops.

Nothing.

Three strides took him up the stoop's narrow stairs, key in hand.

He didn't need it.

The door slid open easily with a touch of his fingers on the knob.

Gingerly Carter stepped inside, rescuing Wilhelmina from her holster under his left arm.

To his right was a small, cozy sitting room; to the left was a dining room. Neither room was expensively furnished, but both reeked of good taste done with a woman's hand in a Moorish-Mediterranean style.

The hall between the rooms led to a large kitchen, and beyond that a small rear courtyard was surrounded by a stone fence and wild with lush bougainvillea. The white tile floor of the kitchen was spotless, as were the cabinets and hanging copperware nearly obscuring the ceiling.

Back in the hall, Carter moved up a narrow stairwell to the second floor bedrooms. A wide corridor fitted with a crimson carpet runner ran the length of the hall.

There were three doors, all closed.

Carter tried the first. The knob turned easily and he pushed it with his foot, tightening his finger on the trigger of the Luger.

The room was empty.

The second one wasn't.

It was a bedroom, and on the bed was a woman. It didn't take too much deduction on Carter's part to figure out the woman's identity. She was still dressed in the red and gold skirt and white, full-sleeved blouse.

That is, what was left of the blouse and skirt.

Both garments were pretty much in tatters and covered with blood. Her breasts, belly, and the sides of her neck sported what looked like cigarette burns. There were long red lines down her arms and legs, probably caused by a very keen-edged knife.

The coup de grâce had been administered by a tassled gold cord pulled from a nearby window drape.

Now Carter knew how the shooters had found him and Jorge and Leonita.

Yes, he thought, moving back down the stairs, these boys were playing for very high stakes.

He found the telephone in the kitchen.

"*Sim*, Senhor Carter, one moment."

It was more like ten seconds.

"Avila here. That you, Carter?"

"It is."

"My man Pepe will never be the same."

"Sorry about that. You should have told me you were putting him on me."

"I know that now. Any luck?"

"A little . . . bad and good. You know Rua Espronza, just on the seaward side of the Alfama?"

"I know it."

"I'm at number eight . . . with a body. She's Leonita Silva's maid. A couple of Algerian shooters did her in trying to find out where Jorge Silva was."

"And did they find out?"

"Yeah," Carter replied with a sigh. "He's dead, too."

There was a long silent pause from the other end of the line, followed by a slight gnashing of teeth before Miguel Avila spoke again.

"I hope your business in my country comes to an end soon, Carter."

"So do I. In the meantime, can you handle the mess here? The local police might ask too many questions."

"I'll have to ask some myself, get a statement."

"That's fine, but make it as fast as possible. I've got to move. It shouldn't be too much of a problem . . . what we call in the States an 'open and shut case.' "

"How so?"

"I'm positive the shooters did it, and I can tell you right where to find them."

"Will they stay put?" Avila asked.

"You have my word on it," Carter replied with a mirthless chuckle.

Nick Carter drove the Cortina hard, so it was just after dusk when they neared Sagres, where the Atlantic Ocean and the Mediterranean Sea come together at Cape St. Vincent.

Normally, in such a situation, he would have searched for a small inn or a hotel in an out-of-the-way, obscure place. But now he threw caution to the winds.

For one reason, when the shooters didn't report in, "the man"—as Carter had started calling him in his mind— would know that something had gone wrong.

For a second reason, Carter's body was talking to him. He wanted a very hot bath, a tall cool scotch, a gourmet meal, and a clean, comfortable bed.

At the Vila do Bispo turnoff, Carter broke the silence that had been hanging between them for the last forty-five miles.

"Do you know the Pousada do Infante?"

"*Sim,*" Leonita nodded. "It is very nice."

"Which road? I've forgotten."

She gave directions, and fifteen minutes later Carter halted the Cortina in front of a huge, whitewashed structure with a red-tiled roof, Moorish arches, and phony minarets dotting the roofs.

"A mile from here is a tiny hotel on the beach . . . much cheaper," Leonita said.

"Cost is no object," Carter smiled, helping her from the car. "There are certain advantages to expense accounts, and Uncle Sam is fifty thousand in front!''

To make his point, Carter patted his belly where he still wore the money belt. A cloud darkened her gaze, and Carter immediately regretted his words.

"I'm sorry, Leonita. I wasn't thinking."

"No matter," she shrugged. "It is true."

They made a handsome couple walking into the spacious wood and tile lobby. Carter had discarded his fisherman's garb and now wore the summer dress of a tourist: white shoes, matching tan shirt and slacks, and a lightweight beige jacket.

His tanned skin was nearly as dark as hers, and he hadn't rinsed the blue-black dye out of his hair, nor had he removed the heavy black mustache from his upper lip.

Leonita was dressed in a lightweight three-piece traveling suit. The whiteness of the snug skirt, the blouse, and the jacket emphasized the dark gold of her skin and the thick halo of her raven hair.

At first glance they could have been an affluent Spanish or Portuguese couple on vacation.

This was fine with Carter. Whoever "the man" was, he surely knew they were coming—from somewhere, sometime—but there was no need to advertise the fact.

"We have no reservations," Leonita whispered from the side of her mouth. "It will be difficult to obtain a room."

"*A* room?" Carter said, one eyebrow lifting into his forehead.

"*Sim*," she replied noncommittally. "Let me do the inquiry."

She was alternately beguiling and demanding as she spoke to the pousada's concierge in rapid Portuguese laced with the southern Algarve dialect.

The man was a bit pompous and stiff, but under her barrage of words and charm, he seemed to relent.

"They can only give us a suite," she told Carter in a low voice.

"Take it," he replied, "and have drinks, some figs, and almond sweets sent up."

She nodded and turned back to the man behind the wide, polished cypress counter.

Two minutes later they were walking toward the elevator, an ancient bellman ambling behind them with the bags.

"He didn't seem too happy."

"He wasn't. The pousada has been booked up for months with advance reservations."

"Then how did you manage it without passing him a handful of escudos?"

"That would have done little good," Leonita replied, frowning. "Baksheesh is rare in Portugal."

"How then?"

"I told him you were a very important official with the American embassy in Lisbon. The power of government officials—that they understand very well!"

In the elevator, the bellman pushed the button for the third floor, the top floor of the pousada.

"Did he question the two of us in just one suite?"

"Of course not. Why should he? I told him we had just gotten married this morning!"

The suite was traditional, with lots of tile, wall tapestries, and parquet floors, but it was also beautifully and tastefully furnished.

The sitting room was spacious, with high, wide French windows overlooking the ocean and Cape St. Vincent in the distance. The sun was just setting, and the view was breathtaking.

Both the bedroom and bath were large and starkly done in marble and tile in muted colors of the earth and sea.

"Does the suite meet with your approval?" Leonita asked, slipping the linen jacket from her shoulders and making it disappear into a closet.

"Excellent," Carter replied. "I couldn't ask for more at the end of a weary drive."

"Good," she said, moving back into the sitting room in response to a light tap on the door.

Seconds later she returned with a well-stocked tray of drinks and hors d'oeuvres.

"One bed," Carter said tonelessly, tipping the bellboy.

"*Sim,*" she replied with what Carter could only surmise as a cunning smile. "But it is a very large one."

The bellboy bowed his way out, and Leonita deftly fixed drinks.

"Water and ice?" she asked, holding up the whiskey bottle.

"*Sim.* How did you know?"

"You are American," she said, splashing bottled water into the glass and handing it to him.

She poured a glass of wine for herself and then raised it in a toast.

"Tomorrow is for revenge," she said solemnly. "Tonight, we will forget."

"I couldn't have said it better," Carter replied. "*Saúde.*"

They both drank, and Carter headed for the bathroom.

"Right now, if you don't mind, I could use the rejuvenation of a shower."

"Take your time."

He stripped, poured another generous slug of scotch down his throat, and stepped into the steamy shower.

The hot water pouring over him in biting needles immediately gave the taut muscles of his back and shoulders much needed relief. The steel spring that had been wound tightly in his belly for the last two days also seemed to uncoil.

He was just rinsing a mound of shampoo from his hair when he heard the shower door being slid open behind him. Rubbing water from his eyes with the knuckles of his index fingers, Carter whirled.

She stood, nude, on the other side of the mammoth tub. Water bouncing from his shoulders lightly sprayed her body, making her olive skin gleam.

Her breasts were full and high, defying gravity by their curve and shape. The nipples were large, of a darker hue, their sheen from the water like two beacons drawing Carter's eyes.

The rest of her body was a portrait of silky skin and curved perfection. She took two steps closer to him, and her full, sensuous lips parted, but she didn't speak. Her new position allowed the water spraying from his shoulders to cascade over her head and soak her black hair. It flattened around her head like a helmet, oddly taking years from her usually stern features.

"I was just thinking," Carter whispered huskily, "how full of surprises you are."

Then he realized that tears were rolling steadily down her cheeks. He opened his arms and she came willingly between them.

"Outside I show no fear," she said. "But inside I am full of fear, and anger, and hate. These people who do these things in my country are very bad people. We Portuguese are not a violent people. Even when we make the revolution, we do it with flowers in the barrels of our rifles."

"I know," Carter said, drawing her closer to him.

"But I will help you, Nick. I will be your eyes and your ears here in the Algarve. And I will help you in the end as well, when the time comes."

Carter knew exactly what she meant.

"But as I have said, that is tomorrow. For tonight, hold me!"

"I'll do a lot more than that," Carter growled, feeling the satin smoothness of her skin and the heat of her breath and body as she molded herself against him.

He kissed her very hard, and she didn't seem surprised. She pushed against him, crowding him to the tiled wall until both of them were under the shower head, the water beating down upon their bodies, enveloping them in a cocoon of heat.

As her hands moved over him, Carter's skin rippled and

his body responded. She became an amazingly adept creature of softness and tenderness. Yet Carter could sense the welling passion in her body as his own hands moved down her back and over the supple arc of her buttocks.

Her lips left his to find his ear, and then he heard her crooning voice.

She was singing the fado, muted, the words barely a whisper, with her lips pressed against his ear.

Carter had made love to many women, but he could never remember the foreplay ever being so erotic.

He listened, letting the timbre of her voice invade his soul until he could stand no more.

With one hand he opened the shower door and scooped her into his arms. Without bothering to shut off the water, he stepped from the tub and, with both of them still soaking wet, carried her into the bedroom.

As they tumbled together onto the bed, the crooning in her voice stopped. It was replaced with words, both in English and Portuguese. They were words of passion and desire, but Carter didn't hear them. He could only hear the pounding of his own desire, not unlike the waves that crashed against the rocks outside and far below the suite's open windows.

Leonita willingly opened her arms and legs to his touch and drew him into her.

Suddenly the serene, still waters inside her turned into pounding surf. Her body became a volcano of heat and motion.

Her eyes, beneath his, were tightly closed and her lips were curled back, exposing her white, even teeth. Her neck and body were arched as her lower lip disappeared between her teeth.

Again and again her velvet warmth grasped his throbbing manhood as they meshed their bodies in the rising tide of passion.

Carter knew that he was riding her to the end when she began answering his every thrust with bone-jarring jolts from her own hips and pelvis.

When they reached the peak, her legs and arms locked around him like twin, fleshy vises. Seconds later, they both exploded.

A sobbing moan came from deep in the back of her throat, quickly followed by a long groan of release from Carter.

They lay still for several moments, their hearts throbbing in unison.

Then Carter pushed himself an arm's length above her and smiled down into her wide, darkly lustrous eyes.

Her long, starkly black hair was fanned out over the pillow behind her head, and the olive curves of her shoulders and breasts glistened with perspiration from both their bodies.

"You are like a gentle animal," she murmured. "I like that."

"And you are a woman," he sighed, feeling himself already beginning to swell again as her agile body began to move.

The Pousada do Infante was spread along the top of a red limestone cliff that seemed to jut right out over the ocean. From the terrace, where they were having a pre-dinner drink, Carter could see oceangoing freighters rounding the point of Cape St. Vincent and heading out into the Atlantic.

Idly he wondered if this would be one of the nights that small fishing boats would be setting out from Portimão or some other village along the Algarve to meet one of these freighters.

"You seem far away," Leonita said from the chaise next to him.

"Just wondering if the shrimp are running off Sagres," Carter said.

She replied with a nod. "I know. I was thinking the same."

"Shall we go in? My nose is telling my belly that it's time to eat."

They stood and moved toward the line of glass doors that led to the inn's dining room.

"That is truly a beautiful sight," Leonita said, pausing at the stone rail of the terrace and gazing down into the harbor.

Carter followed her gaze. A three-masted schooner was moving into the harbor under full sail. She was white, with a gleaming fresh coat of paint and gold leaf trim.

As they watched, the schooner's skipper whirled the one-hundred-foot boat around into the wind. Ready hands were instantly at the sails, and in no time the sleek craft was rolling gently at anchor, her sails furled.

"He's good," Carter said, "whoever he is."

The spacious dining room walls were lined from floor to ceiling with colorful tiles, and the furniture was provincial Portuguese.

Carter requested and got a table by one of the tall windows, and ordered a bottle of red wine from the local Lagoa winery.

"You have spent a great deal of time in Portugal, haven't you, Nick?" Leonita said, sipping and studying his face over the rim of her glass.

"Not really, no more than in any other country."

"The last time? Were you here on holiday or business?"

"A holiday," he replied. "With a woman."

"Your wife?"

"I've never been married."

"That is good."

"Oh?"

"Yes. In your line of business I think it would be very bad to be married."

Carter smiled over the rim of his own glass. Once again his estimation of this woman had gone up a few more points. In her own way she was telling him that the lovemaking they had just so wildly enjoyed together was without strings: an affair of the here and now, with no involvement tomorrow.

The dinner was from the sea and perfectly prepared. They ate clams cooked with spicy sausage—*chouriço*—and bacon, followed by squid fried in its own ink and stuffed with *chouriço*, onion, garlic, and tomato.

They were just finishing their coffee when three men entered the dining room. From habit, Carter gave all three a quick once-over. From the way the first one was dressed—a yachting cap and white linen suit—and the way the maître d' gushed over him, Carter guessed they were from the schooner that he and Leonita had seen sailing into the harbor earlier.

He was about to dismiss them when something odd struck him about the yachtsman's two companions. They were both tall, with gaunt cheeks and hollow eyes that seemed to dart everywhere at once. To Carter they looked more like bodyguards than mere dinner companions.

This was confirmed when the maître d' seated them five tables away, directly behind Leonita. As one of them slid into his chair, his coat brushed aside and Carter could see a holster and what looked like the butt of a Beretta.

Who were they and what were they doing here, Carter wondered, and then he told himself that he was just paranoid. Every wealthy man in Europe these days traveled with a bodyguard.

Still, he let his gaze travel to the short, heavily jowled man in the yachting outfit. His eyes were indented deep in his fat face, and his black eyebrows were so bushy they could be combed. He wore a heavy mustache, and the rest of his face could have used a shave.

Carter was about to look away when the man's eyes found his. Suddenly he was half smiling, letting his eyes go up and down lazily as he looked at Carter. Then his gaze rolled to Leonita, and the smile broadened.

"Is something wrong?" Leonita asked.

"No, I don't think so," Carter replied. "It's just that one of the men behind you seems awfully interested in us."

Even as Carter spoke, the three men stood and walked toward the dining room's seaward-side exit. The maître d' rushed to them, obviously frightened out of his wits that the service had been too slow to suit them and they were leaving because of it.

"It's okay," Carter said. "They're leaving."

Leonita swiveled her head around just before the men disappeared through the door. Just as quickly she looked back at Carter. Her eyes were flashing, and they had grown as wide as saucers. Though it seemed impossible, her face had become two shades lighter than its normal olive hue.

"Now it's my turn to ask you," Carter said. "Is something the matter?"

"That man in the yachting hat . . ."

"Yes?"

"That's José Paragem."

Carter stood in the darkness of the room, smoke trailing from the corner of his mouth as he gazed out the window. In the bay below, the schooner's sails belched full with wind and the boat started moving.

"They're leaving," he said, extinguishing his cigarette in an ashtray on the sill before him.

"Are they?" replied Leonita from the bed.

"Good thought. At least the boat is leaving." Carter lit another cigarette and leaned against the side of the window. He turned his body so that he could watch the ship and still see her out of the corner of his eye. "Who were the two with Paragem?"

"One is called Nikko. I don't know the other's name. I know little of them other than that they are both Americans and they went to work for Paragem about a year ago.''

''Just about the time the operation swung into high gear. Are you sure they're American?''

''Yes,'' she replied. ''They are of Italian extraction, but I know that they are American.''

Carter watched the schooner clear the harbor mouth and then bear left. Probably, he guessed, back to Portimão. When he could no longer see the sails, he mashed out the half-finished cigarette and moved to the bed. As he slid in beside Leonita, his hand brushed her naked thigh.

There was no response, and Carter was glad. At the moment there was far too much on his mind.

He lay, looking up into the darkness for several moments, thinking, laying out a plan of attack, and then he spoke.

''Leonita . . .?''

''*Sim?*''

''Do you know a fisherman, with a boat, anywhere in the Algarve, that you can trust?''

''*Sim*, I know of such a man. His name is Fernando de Logales. He lives near the village of Carvoeiro.''

''And you can trust him.''

''With my life.''

''How can you be sure?''

She rolled to her side and raised her body on an elbow until she could look down into Carter's eyes.

''Because Fernando de Logales is my husband.''

FIVE

The place was called the Long Bar. It was located just off the square on Carvoeiro's main street. The street was the main street by virtue of being the only street. And even it was pure, hard-packed clay rutted with potholes.

Carter adjusted his eyes from the exterior's blazing sun and found a table far in the rear.

"What'll ya have, mate?"

"A beer . . . local. English?"

"Yeah," came the reply, and then he added with a chuckle, "every restaurant and bar in town is owned by an Englishman or Dutchman. We're all sun worshippers!"

"And English tax evaders?" Carter replied, smiling.

"You could say that."

"Make that two beers. I'm expecting someone."

"Right-o, mate."

The beer was cold and welcome. Carter had spent the better part of the morning trudging along the beaches, cliffs, and caves of the Algarve, from the town of Portimão east to the resort area south of Albufeira.

It was only a distance of about twenty-five miles, but in that twenty-five miles Carter had rooted out over a hundred places where a boat could slip in and out completely undetected under cover of darkness.

And that was only a quarter of the length of the Algarve,

which stretched from Cape St. Vincent at the Atlantic to the Spanish frontier.

Carter was just raising the last of his beer when one of the biggest men he had ever seen bent his head to step through the Long Bar's front door.

The man's arms hung like two hairy logs from a short-sleeved checkered shirt, and his legs, encased in a pair of worn jeans, were equally impressive. A mane of black curls was barely held down by a fishing cap, and the jeans were stuffed into the tops of rubber boots.

As he thudded across the bar's wooden floor toward him, Carter thought he resembled a barrel of spikes encased in the hairy skin of a black bull. Only bulls don't chew cigars. He had one about eight inches long and as black as his hair stuck in the side of his mouth. His teeth seemed to worry it harder with each step he took toward the table where Carter sat.

"*Bom dia.*"

"*Bom dia,*" Carter replied, something in the man's scowling face telling him not to stand and offer his hand. "Fernando de Logales?"

"*Sim.* Senhor Carter?"

Carter nodded, and the man eased his bulk into the chair opposite him. Carter could almost hear the wood and rattan of the chair creak in objection to the giant's weight.

"*O senhor fala inglês?*" Carter asked.

"*Não . . . um pouco,*" he said and shrugged his massive shoulders in reply.

"*Francês?*"

"*Oui,*" he nodded.

With a method of communication established, Carter motioned toward the second beer and told de Logales in French that he had ordered it for him.

The giant drained the bottle in two swallows and waved the Long Bar's English owner over with two fingers.

"Now I'm buying," he said when the two fresh bottles had been placed before them.

For several moments the two men sat silently, sipping the beer and testing and weighing each other with their eyes. At last Carter put his elbows on the table and leaned forward.

"How well do you know the coast of the Algarve, Fernando?"

"As well as I know the fish that swim in the sea beside it," the big man growled. "And I am the best fisherman in Portugual."

"How much did Leonita tell you?"

"That a rich American would like to lease the services of myself and my boat. That is all."

"Can you trail another boat at night without being detected?"

"If there is no moon and if the sea is rolling enough . . . yes, it can be done."

So much for part one, Carter thought, lighting a cigarette. *Now we'll see if he will go along with the rest of it.*

"When the time comes, I want to follow a boat on its run in after the catch. It might have to be done several times before I find the right boat."

"And when you do?"

"I want to overtake it at sea and pirate it."

The giant didn't blink. In fact, he didn't even move beyond raising the bottle of beer to his lips.

"Leonita says you are an honest man."

"Most of the time," Carter said.

"What happens to my fellow fishermen on the boat?"

"Nothing, I hope. My guess is they won't be armed, so there will be no reason for any harm to come to them, other than perhaps a few bruises."

"And the pay?"

"Consider the price of a full day's catch for each day of your employ. Is that fair enough?"

For the first time since he had sat down at the table, Fernando smiled. It was a wide, toothy smile that was more like a leer of anticipation.

"I think we'll do business," he said.

"Good. There's one more thing I want you to do."

"*Sim?*"

"Do you know José Paragem?"

The smile disappeared, and for a moment Carter was sure the cigar would snap in half as the man's jaw clamped shut.

"Paragem is a whore and the son of bastards and whores."

"I need a list of all the boats and fishermen he has under lease. Can you get it?"

"I can, but it will take some time."

"How much time?"

"Three, perhaps four days. His boats are home-ported clear to Faro."

"Get it. As soon as you have it, we move. Do you have shortwave on your boat?"

"No."

"I'll get you one," Carter replied, and he slid a thick envelope across the table. Without a word the envelope disappeared inside de Logales's shirt, and he stood.

"Where do I contact you?"

"Vale do Lobo. I'm registered under my own name."

De Logales grunted and exited much as he had entered, shaking the whole bar with each step.

"Another beer, mate?"

"No thanks," Carter replied, dropping a fistful of escudos on the table. "Another time."

He slipped a pair of sunglasses into place and walked out into the sunlight. To his right he saw Fernando de Logales's huge bulk heading toward the beach.

Now Carter believed Leonita that the man could be trusted. As for any problems because of their splintered marriage, she had already put Carter's mind to rest on that score.

They had been very young. Their marriage had been a holdover from days gone past, an arrangement between their families and beyond their control. After two years of living under the same roof as strangers, they had mutually decided that they would separate.

Because of religious reasons, there could be no divorce. Carter guessed that there were other, deeper reasons, but he hadn't pried and Leonita hadn't offered.

Carter watched Fernando wade out to a bobbing boat. It was a sleek, well-cared-for twenty-five-footer, with a single mast and a big Mercury outboard engine. The bow and bottom were wide, so it wouldn't be much for speed.

But then, Carter reasoned, speed wouldn't be a factor. The man's knowledge of the sea would.

When he heard the outboard start up and saw the little boat head out toward the mouth of the bay, Carter turned left up the dusty street.

He had parked the Cortina in an alley two blocks up from the Long Bar. Two steps around the corner, he came up short.

Nikko and his cohort were leaning calmly against the Cortina's front fenders. Like two clones they lounged, with their arms folded over their chests, their thick lips pasted in matching smiles over gleaming white teeth.

"Did you boys lose something?" Carter growled, walking forward until he was only a couple of steps from them.

"We did, but we found it again . . . you."

"Nikko?" Carter asked the speaker.

He nodded and inclined his head to his compatriot partially perched on the opposite fender. "Carlo."

"Nice to meet you both," Carter said, moving to the driver's side door. "Have a nice day."

"Mr. Paragem would like to have a little talk with you, Carter," Nikko said, rolling off the fender and coming up on Carter's left side.

"Don't know the man," Carter said, opening the door a couple of feet with his left hand and resting his right on the top of the car.

Out of the corner of his eye, Carter saw Carlo move along the opposite side of the car.

Foolish move, Carter thought. These two might guard bodies, but they were amateurs when it came to taking one.

"Just a little friendly discussion at Mr. Paragem's villa, Carter," Nikko said. "Why don't you just get in the car nice and quiet, and Carlo and I won't have to get mean."

Carlo was opening the door on the passenger's side. Nikko was unfolding his arms. His right hand held the Beretta that had been hidden by his left bicep.

He never got time to level the gun.

Carter pushed off with his right hand and slammed the door against Nikko. The top sill caught him flush in the face. The door itself jammed the Beretta into his gut. As Nikko fell back, Carlo roared over the front seat, making a grab for Carter with both hands. Carter shifted his grip to the outside of the door and, timing Carlo's lunge, slammed it over the man's wrists.

"You son of a bitch!" Carlo screamed and writhed on the seat in pain.

Carter whirled just in time to meet Nikko's charge.

He'd lost the Beretta in the dust beside the car but came on anyway, fast.

His hands were balled, the thumbs out and protruding forward. They were meant for Carter's eyes, just as the knee coming up hard was meant for his balls.

Carter lowered his head and turned his hip to take the knee.

Nikko, like his clone, cursed with pain when his stiffened thumbs made contact with the top of Carter's skull. There was a sharp, cracking sound, and Carter knew that one, and maybe both, of the man's thumbs had broken.

Carter dipped to one knee and came up with the heel of

his hand, like a hydraulic drill, on the point of Nikko's chin. There was a gurgled grunt as his head snapped back and his teeth ground together.

Just as he was falling backward, Carter grabbed his ears and yanked his head forward. At the same time, he again lowered his own head. When soft face came against hard skull, there was a sickening sound.

Carter released Nikko and watched his pupils roll up into his head as his body rolled back to hit the dusty street with a thud.

He spun just in time to see a cursing Carlo scramble from the car. Both his wrists were badly bruised, but he had managed somehow to paw his own automatic weapon from beneath his armpit.

He held it shakily above his head, planning on implanting the barrel in Carter's skull.

When he made his play, Carter calmly stepped forward and drop-kicked him in the right knee. The gun fell from Carlo's faltering hands and they, in turn, groped reflexively for the smashed kneecap.

With his right knee in the air, Carlo hopped on his left until his back slammed against the Cortina.

"Had enough?" Carter rasped.

"Screw you!"

Carter brought his foot up and then down. The sole of his shoe grated along the other's shinbone until it went all the way down.

Carter was sure the sound of the bones cracking in the man's instep could be heard all the way back to the Long Bar.

With neither leg able to hold his weight, Carlo's butt slid down the Cortina to settle in the dust.

Carter gathered the hardware and then the bodies. He stuffed Nikko's inert frame in the back seat, and then carried a whining Carlo around the car and set him in the front passenger seat.

"You bastard," he moaned. "You broke it."

"What?"

"My goddamn knee."

"I know," Carter grinned. "I also smashed your goddamn foot. But you're lucky."

Without another word, Carter moved back around the car and crawled into the driver's seat.

As he pulled out of the alley, he smiled to himself. An entire battle had been waged, and not one soul had seen a thing.

Carlo and Nikko had picked siesta time to do their snatch.

They had never dreamed that it would work in Carter's favor as much as theirs.

"Directions!" Carter said to the groaning creature beside him.

"Huh . . .?"

"Directions to Paragem's villa," he barked. "I've decided to accept his invitation after all."

"Jesus."

"Yeah. Shame you guys weren't more polite. If you would have said 'please,' you might be in one piece now."

The pink villa was located halfway between Carvoeiro and Portimão, on a cliff jutting out five hundred feet above the ocean. From the road, two hundred yards away, it was partially obscured by lush vegetation and a tall stone fence.

"Yes?" came the voice from an intercom box beside the tall, wrought-iron gate.

"Carlo."

The static in the box went off and the electronically controlled gate swung open silently.

Carter wound his way through the lush garden and around tall eucalyptus trees to a squat, two-story structure that seemed to ramble all over the cliff top.

Carter braked the Cortina in front of a pair of massive, carved oak doors and got out. He moved around the car, cupped his hands, and yelled toward the upper windows.

"Paragem . . . José Paragem!"

A full minute passed, and then a pair of French doors opened just above him. José Paragem, all in white, which emphasized his huge belly, stepped out onto the balcony.

"What do you want?" he asked, sweat dripping from his chin and an obvious quiver in his voice.

"You sent for me, Paragem," Carter replied.

There was no reply, and Carter didn't wait for one. He turned and yanked both doors of the Cortina wide. Nikko came first, his head thudding on the drive when Carter dropped him. Carlo quickly followed, loudly screaming in pain with every move.

When they were both sprawled at Carter's feet, he again looked up toward the balcony.

"Have someone gather up this trash. I think we should talk."

Paragem nodded dumbly and waved his fingers on the end of a shaking left hand toward Carter's right.

"There is a gate in the wall. I shall meet you by the pool."

Carter found the gate and moved through. Over his shoulder he saw four white-coated servants lifting a screaming Carlo and a dead-to-the-world Nikko.

The back of the villa, even though it was also pink, was a little more impressive than the front, with lots of balconies and large, shaded windows.

The pool and adjoining pool house were on the very edge of the cliff, with only a low stone balustrade between them and the rocks below.

Paragem stood beside a chaise, nervously twirling a drink in his hand and watching Carter approach with darting eyes.

Beyond Paragem, Carter saw a bundle of brown skin, black hair, and gleaming teeth. She was short, very compact, and much more of her was oozing out of the tiny bikini than was being held in.

"I believe you sent for me?" Carter said.

"Yes. One moment." He turned to the girl. "Ines, leave us!" he barked in Portuguese.

"*Sim,*" she replied and unwound from her chaise.

As well endowed as she was in all areas, she was still young, not much over seventeen, if she was that.

But she moved like a woman, every inch of her working as she strolled up the veranda steps and into the villa.

"Sit, *senhor.*"

Carter ignored the indicated chair and moved around until his back was to the sea.

"What happened?"

"One of them—Nikko, I think—pulled this . . ."

Carter set the Beretta on the table and held up the other automatic.

"Carlo dropped this after I broke his wrists, a kneecap, and all the bones in one of his feet."

José Paragem paled visibly, and Carter could hear the ice shake in his glass. He set the automatic down beside the Beretta, leaned back with a sigh, and pulled his cigarette case from his jacket pocket.

"The fools . . ."

"What was it you wanted to see me about?"

The slobbering lips came together, and through the fat, Carter could see the muscles of the other man's jaw clenching and unclenching.

"I saw you last night, in Sagres, with Leonita Silva."

"I know."

"Are you . . . uh, friends?"

"You could say that," Carter replied, nodding the cigarette to flame.

"I was surprised to see Leonita back on the Algarve. I was wondering if her brother had returned with her . . . Jorge Silva."

"Why are you interested?"

"Jorge Silva was in my employ at one time. He left rather abruptly with some . . . merchandise . . . that belonged to me."

"Like what?" Carter said, expelling a cloud of smoke.

"That's rather private."

"Is it? Then anything I know about his whereabouts is also private."

Paragem shrugged. "All right . . . for now. Why are you in the Algarve, Senhor Carter?"

"Vacation. I've heard the golf at the Vale do Lobo is some of the most challenging in the world."

"You hardly look like a golfer, Senhor Carter, and Nikko and Carlo are, shall we say, very professional at what they do. I think it would take someone far more professional to do to them what you have just done."

"Then, Senhor Paragem," Carter growled, leaning forward in his chair, "why don't we do away with the smokescreen and say what we both mean?"

The sweat had soaked through Paragem's shirt now, and even though he was under the wide beach umbrella, he looked as though he would rather be in the air-conditioned villa.

"Very well," he said at last, freshening his drink from a silver shaker on the table. "Perhaps it is best that you have taken my two watchdogs out of earshot."

"Your watchdogs? Nikko and Carlo?"

"Yes, what did you think they were?"

"Your bodyguards."

Paragem's jowls waggled in a mirthless laugh. "No, Senhor Carter, I am afraid that it is just the opposite. They have instructions that, should I falter in my part of the bargain in any way, I am to be hung over that balustrade . . . there . . . and dropped, accidentally, onto the rocks below."

Carter hid his confusion behind his cigarette. "Bargain?"

"Yes, a bargain I made two years ago. But first . . . are you with the American government?"

Carter weighed answering, then nodded. "In a way."

Paragem himself nodded, and his knuckles, gripping

the glass, grew white. "I knew they would send someone else. And if you are disposed of, another will come."

"Ramon Alvarez?"

"Yes."

"Is he dead?"

"I assume he is. I am only told what is necessary for me to know in order to complete my part of the business."

"Suppose you tell me what the bargain is that you have, and with whom you have it?"

Paragem nervously sipped his drink and let his eyes float out over the balustrade to the sea. It was obvious to Carter that here was a man who had gotten in far over his head and now wanted out.

The problem that showed in his eyes and sweaty face was obvious: Did he have the guts to try?

"A little over two years ago, a woman approached me in Tangier. She knew of my various activities . . ."

"Smuggling?"

"Among other things."

"What other things?" Carter pushed.

"That isn't important." Carter made a movement to rise. "No . . . wait, I will answer you. White slavery to the brothels in Rabat and Casablanca. Illegal arms in northern Spain. Heroin, hashish, cocaine in Marseille. Is that enough?"

"For now. You were a busy man," Carter said, fighting down the revulsion that threatened to boil up in his gut.

With short lapses, Paragem told approximately the same story that Carter had heard from Jorge Silva. He contracted for the boats, got their owners to sail them, and arranged for the pickups at sea.

"Shortly before the operation was to begin, the woman again summoned me to Tangier. She gave me certain codes that would appear biweekly in ads in a Lisbon newspaper. These would tell me what freighters to intercept and when. She also told me that this would be my last contact with her. The operation in Portugal and the transfer of the heroin to its final destination would be handled by someone here in the Algarve.''

"Who?" Carter asked.

"I do not know. All business transactions, instructions—everything—is done by telephone.''

"In Portuguese?"

"No, always in French.''

"Your English is excellent, Paragem. Has this man ever spoken in English to you?''

"No, but his French is accented. It could be English, I can't tell.''

Carter pulled the by now well-thumbed portrait of Coco Chanette from his coat pocket. "Is this the woman who contacted you in Tangier?''

Paragem barely glanced at the photo and nodded. "Yes. She is older now than she appears in this photo, but, yes, it is the same woman.''

Carter made the photo disappear back into his coat and mulled over the next tack he should take with José Paragem.

"Where does the refined heroin go when it leaves the Algarve?'' he asked after a long pause.

"I think, Senhor Carter, you know that or you wouldn't be here.''

Carter smiled. Paragem was being cooperative, but he didn't want to appear *too* cooperative.

"We have reason to believe that it goes to NATO bases around Europe.''

"Most of it does," Paragem said, nodding. "Some stays here to control the market and the price.''

"Where?" Carter asked, feeling ripples of anticipation curl up and down his spine.

"I don't know that either," Paragem replied, doing his best to return Carter's penetrating stare and failing miserably.

"We have a saying in the States, Paragem . . . bullshit.''

"I swear I don't know . . . at least, all of it. The boats are off-loaded in different places each time."

"I know that."

"The crates are marked so the drivers know where to take them. The crates containing the rock salt and fish are taken to Faro for immediate shipment. The crates of dry ice and fish are distributed to restaurants."

"In other words, dry ice and fish equals no heroin."

"I would assume that."

So far, everything the man had related jived with what Carter already knew, and it seemed to fall in place. But he couldn't shake the feeling that Paragem was leaving something—maybe a lot—unsaid.

"What about the heroin that's warehoused for future use?"

"That comes in a special crate once a month. Where it goes after it's off-loaded, I have no idea."

"What's so special about it?"

Paragem shrugged and Carter didn't push it. At this point, he figured whatever he could get out of this fat man was more than he already had. He would try for more later.

"I take it, Paragem, that you want to change sides?"

"No. I have money, a great deal of money. I want a new identity and papers that will let me into the United States."

"That's a tall order," Carter said. "But I think it can be arranged."

"Good. What do you require of me?"

"When you put out the next call—'the shrimp are running off Sagres'—I will call you. I want the coordinates where the boats meet the freighter."

"Very well." Paragem jotted his private number on a slip of paper and passed it to Carter.

"We might have to make the run two or three times before I hit the boat I want."

"I understand," Paragem wheezed. "Now there is one

thing I need from you. I must know the whereabouts of Jorge Silva. Getting that information will be my cover for the little chat we have had when *he* calls.''

''Jorge Silva is dead. The two shooters you sent to get him, got him.''

There was obvious relief in Paragem's florid face. ''And the two Algerians?''

''I got them.''

''You are truly an amazing man, Senhor Carter. One other thing . . . did Silva give you anything—a package—before he left this world?''

''Your merchandise?''

''Yes. It would help if it could be recovered.''

''Suppose you tell me how Silva got it?'' Carter could pretty well guess what *it* was.

''He obtained it from Ramon Alvarez.''

''Go on,'' Carter said.

''Alvarez did much the same thing that I assume you are planning. He followed a boat in and then hijacked the truck.''

''Where was the truck headed?''

''To Faro . . . for export.''

''You're lying, Paragem.''

''No . . .''

''Yes!'' Carter hissed. ''Let me see if I can't work it out. Alvarez gets Silva to help, offers him a lot of coin for it. Jorge sees a way to collect from both ends. He comes to you. You pay him to set up Alvarez so Chanette can kill him. Only Jorge didn't know he was being set up at the same time . . .''

Carter watched the fat man digest what he had said so far. From the man's facial contortions and physical twitches, Carter guessed he was hitting it about right.

''I would also guess,'' he continued, ''that while Chanette and Alvarez were having it out, Silva cracked one of the crates and lifted a few kilos before he jumped ship. Is that about right, Paragem?''

"Yes," Paragem sighed.

"And *the man* wants those few kilos back . . . bad enough to send shooters all over Portugal to find Silva."

"Yes."

"Why?"

"What?" Paragem's eyes came up, wide with fear now.

"Why, with all the dope that's being run through this operations, is *the man* so concerned about these kilos?"

"If I knew that, Senhor Carter, I would not need to be dealing with you now."

"Fair enough," Carter said, standing, "for now. We'll be in touch."

Without another word, Carter crossed around the pool and made his way to the gate in the stone fence. As he strolled down the drive toward the Cortina, a prickly feeling raised the short hairs on the back of his neck.

It was an instinctive feeling, bred from years of having a pair of eyes watch his every move.

His own eyes darted around the car, the heavy foliage near the entranceway, and along the villa's front wall.

Nothing. *Nada*. At least nothing that breathed or moved or held a weapon.

Then his eyes drifted up.

He was standing on the balcony where Carter had first seen Paragem. Nikko.

Three quarters of his face was swathed in stark white bandages, but Carter had no trouble seeing the burning black eyes.

They spoke to him, saying without words that this particular meeting had only been round one.

Carter figured as much.

When round two came along, Carter knew he would have to kill Nikko; it was either that, or buy the big sleep himself.

They hadn't wired the Cortina with an IRA special, but then Carter didn't figure they would. If Paragem was telling the truth, he would want Carter alive as a new partner. If the fat man were lying, he would still keep Carter alive for the time being until the trap could be sprung.

Carter drove down the long drive and was through the gardens in seconds. When he was twenty yards from the big wrought-iron gates, they swung open and he sped through.

He turned right, back toward Carvoeiro, and was just about to stomp the accelerator, when a flash of black appeared from the tall eucalyptus trees and heavy undergrowth beside the narrow road.

Carter cursed and set the Cortina on its nose.

The front bumper of the car came to a stop inches from an old woman, dressed all in black from head to toe, carrying a tied bundle of faggots on her head.

Carter was about to reach for the door handle when the woman shucked the bundle into the bushes and streaked for the side of the car. Like a cat she was through the rear door and slamming it behind her.

Carter started to tell her in no uncertain terms that this was a weird way to hitchhike, when she huddled down deep into the rear seat and threw the heavy black shawl from her head.

It was the youthful bundle of dancing flesh from beside Paragem's pool, Ines.

"Por favor, senhor! Depressa . . . depressa! . . . É urgente! Por favor, por favor!"

Carter's Portuguese was rudimentary, but he did know that *depressa* meant to hurry, and *urgente* spoke for itself.

He slammed the gear lever into first, hit the gas pedal, and drove away *rapidamente*.

SIX

Nick Carter should have realized when he first spotted Ines by the pool that she was the ''servant'' of Paragems that Jorge Silva had mentioned. He got that much out of the girl on the wild drive across the Algarve to Vale do Lobo.

And that was about all he got.

The girl was a bundle of nerves and so afraid that even her Portuguese rattled out in fragmented sentences and disjointed phrases.

In the hotel parking lot, Carter got her partially calmed down. In his minimal Portuguese, some French, a little English, and a lot of sign language, he instructed her to enter the hotel behind him and head immediately for the ladies room in the lobby. She was to wait there fifteen minutes, and then take the elevator to the second floor. From the second floor she was to take the stairs to the fourth.

He would be waiting for her in Suite 414.

All this took an agonizing fifteen minutes, which left Carter wringing wet with perspiration.

He only hoped, as he entered the lobby, that she had understood. If Paragem or *the man* had eyes on him, they were probably in the hotel itself. In the traditional black peasant dress, Ines's youth would be hard to spot, and, hopefully, by taking such a roundabout route to his suite, she would completely elude detection.

Carter stayed unhurried and casual as he moved across the gaudy marble and tile lobby to the desk.

"Four-fourteen . . . any messages?"

"*Sim*, Senhor Carter, one moment."

His hand dived into the box marked 414 and came out with two pink slips of paper.

"*Obrigado*," Carter mumbled and headed for the elevator.

The first message was from Leonita: *I'm enjoying the pool like the idle rich.*

The second was from David Hawk: *Call home.*

In the suite, Carter poured a shooter of Chivas with one hand and grabbed the phone with the other.

"*Piscina.*"

"Would you page Menina Silva, *por favor?*"

"*Sim, Senhor.* One moment."

The other receiver clanked as if it had been dropped on the floor. Carter let half the shot of Chivas roll down his throat to burn away the nerves in his belly, then answered the now familiar voice.

"It's me. Get your beautiful self up to the suite right away."

"Something?"

"Yeah, I need an interpreter."

Carter replaced the receiver, downed the rest of the shot, and poured another.

A light tap on the door brought him across the room in a second.

"Get inside . . . quick!"

Ines darted around him, took in the room like a frightened deer, and then sighed an audible sigh of relief. The shawl dropped to her shoulders and her eyes said many *obrigados* in response to Carter's reassuring smile.

"Drink?" Carter asked, holding up his glass.

She shook her head. "*Água mineral?*"

"*Sim.*"

Carter plopped a couple of cubes into a glass and filled it with bottled water.

When Leonita's key sounded in the door, the girl bolted. If Carter hadn't grabbed her it was no telling what she might have done. Her eyes were already gauging the distance to the windows.

"It's okay, it's all right," Carter said in the most soothing voice he could muster. "*Uma amiga.*"

The sight of another woman calmed Ines more than anything Carter could say. And Leonita was quite a sight. Carter had jammed a roll of escudo notes in her hand that morning and told her to splurge.

She had, and it made quite an eyeful.

A white soft cotton robe came to mid-thigh. The robe's sash was undone, and where it parted Carter could see an equally stark white, very form-fitting one-piece suit. The color made her skin even more golden in contrast, and the fit gave her the body of a goddess.

The twin globes of her breasts above the bra cups arched provocatively, and her long, trim legs flowing from the white suit could have come right off a Vegas line.

"Damn, you're beautiful . . ."

"Thank you," she replied, her forehead furrowed. "But . . .?"

"Oh, yeah. This is Ines. Ines . . . Leonita."

"Leonita Silva?" the girl cried.

"*Sim.*"

The girl flew across the room and threw her arms around Leonita as if she had just found her long-lost sister.

Carter was soon to learn that that was almost the case.

Leonita managed to calm her down and get her seated on one of the two large settees near the windows.

And then it started, a machine-gun-like chatter that made Carter's head spin trying to follow. He barely caught a word here and there, and finally gave up, retreating to the portable bar.

He was pretty sure he was catching question marks on Leonita's side of the conversation, so he could assume she was getting what Carter would want to know.

Twenty minutes later Ines leaned back on the settee, exhausted.

Leonita turned to Nick. *"Good God . . ."*

"Is that all?"

Leonita stood, tugging the girl to her feet. "Let me get her into a bath. She says she's sticky with suntan lotion under those clothes. While she's soaking I'll tell you everything she told me."

Carter could only nod in agreement. There was that much resolution on her face.

He could hear water running and more jabbering between them from the bath as he poured another drink.

The thought flicked briefly across his mind that he was trusting Leonita to indeed tell him everything the girl had told her. Was it safe to trust Leonita that much? Or anyone else for that matter?

He didn't have one hell of a lot of choice.

And then he remembered the message from Hawk: *Call home.*

He was heading for the phone when Leonita emerged from the bedroom. She had slipped out of the swimsuit and into a sheer aqua blouse and a matching pair of slacks.

"I like your taste in clothes."

"I'm glad," she smiled. "It's been a long time since I've been able to indulge."

She saw the look of perplexity on Carter's face, and knew that his mind was on things other than the clothes she had purchased.

"Her name is Ines Vazques."

"She was the servant girl in Paragem's house that your brother seduced, wasn't she?"

"Yes," Leonita replied, the corners of her mouth curling downward with distaste. "Jorge made love to her and promised that he would take her far away from Paragem. He never intended to . . . I know that."

"Did you tell her that?"

"No, I thought it best that I should not until I have told you everything she told me. Neither did I tell her that Jorge is no longer in this world."

"Probably wise," Carter nodded, rolling the glass between his fingers. "Okay, let's get with it . . . brief me."

"What?"

"Tell me," he said, correcting the slang she obviously didn't understand.

"She has been with José Paragem for almost a year, since just after he bought the villa. Her parents are dead. Paragem bought her from an uncle in the north."

"Legally?"

"Of course not," Leonita snapped. "But such things can be done illegally, and there is little the victim can do about it. Also, the girl has no education so that she would know the difference. She can barely read or write."

"I see your point. Go on."

"Ines functioned as just a maid for a while at the villa. But then Paragem took note of her physical attributes, and she was promoted . . . if you can call it that."

"And she had no choice."

"None. The alternative would have been a brothel in Morocco or Algeria, or worse, a camel driver's concubine in the Sahara. He held this threat constantly over her head, so that when Jorge came along, she was ready to listen and believe anything he told her."

"And what information did she supply to your brother?"

"She kept him constantly up-to-date on who visited Paragem at the villa and who he visited when he went out—at least when he would take her along. A few months ago Paragem began to use Ines to distribute the envelopes to fishermen."

"Those would have been the runs and destinations. No wonder Jorge and Alvarez were able to start pinpointing all the action!"

"It would seem so."

"Did she mention any single visitor who came to the villa more often than the others?"

"Two. A small, weasel-faced man and a tall, distinguished man with silvery hair."

"Either of them English or American?"

"No, at least she doesn't think so. The small man was definitely Portuguese. The tall one she thinks was Spanish. At least he looked Spanish. She never heard him speak."

Carter stood, lighting yet another cigarette as he began to pace.

"When was the last time she saw Jorge?"

"I was coming to that."

Something in her tone made Carter pause and whirl to face her. Leonita was smiling.

"As near as I can figure, it must have been the night he called me in Lisbon . . . or the night before."

"That would have been about the exact time he started his run to escape."

Leonita nodded, and Carter left unsaid the discrepancy between what happened that night on the boat according to Jorge's story and from what Carter had figured out from Paragem's end of it.

"Do you know what a squid lure is?" she asked.

"No."

"All along the cliffs of the Algarve you can find them. It is nothing more than a very large, bare, high-watt bulb hung down over a cliff."

"Yes?"

"They are usually hung at a place where the sea is inaccessible from the top of a cliff. The waters in these areas are usually a little calmer and much deeper than near coves where beaches are. At night, when the bulb is lit and lowered near the sea, the squid are attracted to the light and netted."

"And there is such a place near Paragem's villa?"

"*Sim.* Halfway down the side of the cliff is a cave. To any but an experienced fisherman's eye, the cave would be inaccessible. But there are natural grooves worn into the cliffside from the sea up to the cave. They can be used to climb."

"And that was where they met." Carter could tell that Leonita was building toward something, but he didn't push her.

"Each night, at a certain time, Ines would watch from her window in the villa for the light to come on and blink three times. That was the signal that Jorge was waiting for her. That last night she was surprised that he came. She hadn't expected him."

Carter's muscles tensed as he slid into the settee beside Leonita. His voice when he spoke was raspy.

"Let me see if I can guess. She went to the cave. Jorge was frightened out of his wits. He told her that he had to leave. He was going to Lisbon to get your help. He proclaimed his undying love for Ines, and then he gave her a package to keep for him."

"Yes," she replied, her mouth dropping open in surprise. "How did—"

"I'll tell you later. Where is the package now?"

"I didn't ask her that. I didn't think it was that important. What I thought *was* important was that Jorge told her who I was, and that I would be coming to pick it up."

Good old Jorge strikes again, Carter thought. *After he collects from Paragem and collects from Uncle Sam, he sends his sister to take the risk of the final collection!*

Carter was almost glad the shooters had gotten Jorge. If they hadn't, Carter was pretty sure he himself would have wasted the little rat before all this was over.

"Get her out here," he said. "I think the package may be very important."

Three minutes later a still damp Ines stood before Carter in Leonita's terry cloth robe.

"Ask her."

Ines was calmer now. As she answered Leonita's questions, the quick glances she threw Carter's way were devoid of the fear he had witnessed earlier.

At least Leonita seemed satisfied and turned to Carter.

"After Jorge gave her the package that night, he told her to wait a half hour and then return to the villa. But right after he slipped into the sea she saw one of Paragem's boats—"

"Boats?" Carter asked.

"Yes. He has two powerboats off the yacht patrolling the seaward side of the villa at night."

"Okay, go on."

"Ines saw the boats and became frightened. Jorge had told her to take the package back to the villa and hide it there. But she was afraid, so she hid it right there in the cave and then, when the boats had passed, left at once."

"So the package is still in the cave!"

"*Sim.*"

Carter moved quickly into the bedroom and rummaged in his briefcase. He came up with several tourist folders of Portugal and the Algarve, and leafed through them until he found what he wanted.

Back in the sitting room, he spread what he thought should be a detailed map of the southern coast out in front of Ines.

"Portimão here," he pointed, "Carvoeiro here. Paragem's villa would be about here. Tell her to point out the location of the cave."

Leonita translated and Ines nodded her understanding.

She leaned over the map, her eyes squinted, the forehead of her dark, pretty face furrowed in concentration. One polished nail moved along the map, stopping now and then, only to start again.

Over the bent head, Leonita and Carter exchanged nervous glances.

At least the girl's head came up and she looked bewilderingly at both of them. Carter knew even before she spoke that the map was a lost cause.

Leonita confirmed it when she translated.

"She cannot find the place. This map is too small and there are many cliffs and caves not on it."

"Yeah, I figured."

Carter moved to the bar and made a third drink even though he didn't need it. Silently he sipped and paced until a thought struck him.

"Leonita . . ."

"*Sim?*"

"Have her describe the place to you—every rock, every dip of the terrain, the color of the cliff in that particular spot—everything. Also, the distance by sea and by foot from the villa."

Five minutes later Carter was smiling and rapidly dialing the phone.

"*Sim?*" came a feminine voice.

"Fernando, *por favor*," Carter said. Seconds later, Fernando de Logales's deep bass voice came on the line.

"Fernando, this is your new employer. Do you recognize the voice?"

"*Oui.*"

"I am going to put someone on the line. She will describe a place on the coast between Portimão and Carvoeiro. I hope you will recognize it."

Carter passed the receiver to Ines as Leonita explained to the girl what he wanted.

Carefully, with her eyes shut tightly in concentration, Ines spoke. When she was finished, several questions came from the other end of the line, which she readily answered.

Then she handed the phone back to Carter.

"Do you know the place, Fernando?"

"*Oui.* It is very difficult to reach by boat . . . sandbars and rocks. But there is a cove just to the west. We could anchor there and swim around the point."

"What would be a good time to go there, undisturbed?"

"I would say around midnight."

"Good. Pick me up about fifty meters off the beach at Vilamoura at about eleven. We'll sail back west from there."

"Eleven. I will see you then."

Carter cradled the phone and turned back to face Ines.

"Now we have to do something about you."

"*Sim?*"

"Leonita, tell her about Jorge, and ask her where she would like to go. Anywhere . . . it's on Uncle Sam."

"She has no place to go, Nick," Leonita replied softly. "But I know a place where I think she would be safe."

Unlike the Spanish—who refuse to even open the doors of their restaurants for the evening meal before nine—the Portuguese dine early.

Carter and Leonita were in the dining room promptly at seven. Carter purposely dined light on a fish entree and a salad. Just as purposely, he seemed to consume great amounts of sangria.

By the end of the meal, he was not roaring drunk but he was borderline obnoxious.

From the dining room they moved to the lounge, where he started to consume great amounts of scotch. By nine o'clock the lounge patrons were all too happy to see him stagger out on Leonita's arm.

At the door he bussed her soundly on the lips and proclaimed loudly, "Come along, darling! We'll go back to the suite where you can change into your black robes, and then on to O Vapor where you can sing!"

In the elevator, Carter could barely suppress his laughter; Leonita was clearly mortified.

"Is it so bad?" he whispered.

"Yes," she replied, managing a wan smile. "I will never be able to look anyone in the face again!"

The hall was clear when they stepped from the elevator. Carter at once went into his act. They bypassed the suite and loudly charged down the hall to the floor maid's cubicle.

The old woman answered Carter's pounding with obvious shock and amazement on her face.

"Ice, darling!" Carter shouted, reeling drunkenly on Leonita's shoulder. "Tell the old dear we want ice at once in 414!"

Red-faced, Leonita translated as Carter shoved escudos in the woman's hand.

The maid nodded and headed for the service elevator. The door had barely closed behind her when Carter was in the linen room flipping through a stack of white uniforms, calling out the sizes.

"That one will do."

He shook the uniform out as he stepped back into the cubicle. Leonita had already stripped to bra, panties, and pantyhose. He held the uniform as she stepped into it, and then helped her button it up. Just as quickly her mane of hair went under a Bo Peep-type cap, and then she added sunglasses.

They just reached the door of the suite when the service elevator door started to slide open. Leonita darted into the suite, threw the discarded dress to a waiting Ines, and watched through a crack in the door as Carter lurched toward the elevator.

The maid stepped out, a stainless steel ice bucket clutched to her breasts.

"Dear, ye're a saint," Carter slurred, throwing one arm over her shoulder and groping until his fingers found the power button on the floor panel. "Truly, truly a saint you are!"

He flipped the switch on "off" and maneuvered the woman down the hall. She jabbered her objections and thrust the ice bucket in his direction as they passed the door of 414.

"I know, I know, dear," Carter soothed, "but I need a few fresh towels . . . I'll save you a trip!"

"*O quê?*" she said, thrusting the ice bucket into his waving hand. "*Cubos de gelo!*"

"Yes dear, I know, ice . . . *gelo. Obrigado,*" he

burped, keeping her head forward with his shoulder. "*Obrigado,* a thousand thanks, but I need towels . . . *toalha,* you know?"

"Ah, *toalha!*" she cried, relief written all over her flat, wide face. "*Toalha de banho?*"

"*Sim, sim, sim!*" Carter roared, gently thrusting more escudos into her hands and her body in turn into the linen room.

He saw a flash of white in the hall.

"*Toalhas!*" the maid chirped as her arms filled with a load of bath towels.

"*Sim . . . obrigado,*" he replied, weaving away.

"*Boa sorte!*" she cried after him and flapped her hands in the meaningful gesture of "don't come back."

The service elevator doors slid quietly closed and Carter entered the suite.

Ines was waiting.

Carter caught her wrist and gently turned her around, scrutinizing. The shoes were a shade lighter than Leonita had been wearing, but that wouldn't matter. A man would never notice, and they made Ines nearly as tall as Leonita. The dress, of course, was the same, and the fit was almost perfect.

Leonita had already restyled the girl's hair and placed two roses on the side, in front of one ear, exactly as she had worn them at dinner. The makeup too was like Leonita's, darkly rouged cheeks and heavy scarlet lip gloss.

"Perfect," Carter sighed, slipping a pair of sunglasses over her eyes and a heavy black shawl over her head and shoulders.

He pinned the shawl under her chin so he wouldn't tug it off with his coming antics in the lobby, then checked his watch.

Leonita would be out the service entrance now and around the pool. Another two minutes and she would be passing the ninth hole of the golf course and nearing the beach.

When the two minutes had passed, he put his arm around Ines's shoulders and tested her ability to take some of his weight.

"Okay?" he asked.

"*Sim*," she nodded.

"Good. Let's go!"

The maid was on her stool at the end of the hall. The second she saw them emerge from the door of the suite, she darted into her cubicle and loudly slammed the door behind her.

"So far, so good," Carter breathed.

In the lobby he played the drunk bit down a little, but not so much that everyone wasn't very aware that he and Leonita were leaving for the evening.

He let everyone know their destination by singing an off-key melody through the lobby and all the way to the parking lot.

"O Vapor, we will go . . . O Vapor we will go, high ho the merry o, O Vapor we will go!"

Even as he reeled on Ines's shoulder, Carter kept his eyes alert as they moved through the rows of cars toward the Cortina.

Once there, he made a great show of placing her in the passenger seat and then weaving his way around to the driver's side, all the time still looking.

Carter spotted him in a black Fiesta; a big black with muscular shoulders and a scar that gleamed pink across his cheek. He glanced Carter's way once, and Carter caught it out of the corner of his own eye. The guy had a look in his eyes that would frighten children.

Carter took his time getting the Cortina started and, in a way that would agree with his inebriated state, made several wrong turns before getting out of the parking lot.

When he at last found the gates that led to the main road out of the complex, he again checked the rearview mirror. A figure had darted from the hotel's front entrance

and was now leaning into the Fiesta, speaking to the
black.

He raised up just in time for Carter to recognize the
waiter who had been assigned their table that evening in
the dining room.

Carter led the Fiesta a merry chase for twenty or so
minutes. He stopped at two gas stations and made a great
show of asking directions, went into a roadside bar and
emerged with a beer in hand, and even stopped an old man
on a donkey cart.

Nearly a half hour had passed when Carter at last took
the road that would lead them to the Vilamoura marina and
the O Vapor restaurant.

But, almost there, he charged off on a secondary road
that led through a field of olive and eucalyptus trees.
Carefully he watched the road behind him with the breath
held tightly in his lungs.

Then he saw the lights of the Fiesta flash by and heaved
a sigh of relief.

"O-kay?" Ines asked, mimicking Carter's drawn-out
inflection of the word.

"Okay," he replied with a chuckle.

As he had hoped, the guy in the Fiesta had been informed of their eventual destination by his comrade in the
hotel.

After watching Carter ramble around the countryside
for a half hour, making wrong turns but constantly heading in the right direction, the black had just gone on to O
Vapor to wait for them.

Carter continued on the rutted, dusty road for a little
over a mile, until the lights of Vilamoura village were on
his left. Then he started sighting toward his right where he
knew that somewhere in the darkness was the main east-
west Algarve highway and the landmark he was looking
for.

"Bingo!" he said, emerging from a grove of trees and topping a rise in the road.

Ines pointed. *"Farol?"*

"That's right," Carter said, hitting the asphalt of the main road and turning left. "The lighthouse!"

There are old but still used lighthouses all along the coast of the Algarve. The one on the road leading from the main highway down to Vilamoura was the biggest and whitest of them all.

Carter had barely come to a halt alongside the chain link fence surrounding the huge white structure when Leonita appeared at the window.

"Were you followed?"

Carter nodded, reaching his arm back and opening the rear door for her. Ines was already scrambling into the back seat.

"A big African type," he said. "It went like clockwork. He's probably sitting in the marina parking lot waiting for us right now."

Leonita got into the back seat, already tearing at the buttons on the maid's uniform. Carter caught a glimpse of bare belly and thigh and knew that Ines was nearly stripped.

"You have any trouble?" he asked, searching the road ahead and behind for any lights.

"None," Leonita said.

"Where's the taxi?"

"Back at that *taberna* you passed off the main road."

"Tell her," he said.

Leonita did, in quick, terse sentences, as Carter passed escudo notes to the girl over the seat.

Both of them emerged from the car on opposite sides and met in the rear. They embraced, and Ines, now dressed in white and still wearing the dark glasses, began walking back toward the bar up the road.

Leonita crawled into the passenger seat, leaned over,

and passionately kissed Carter on the lips.

"What was that for?"

"For her," Leonita replied. "You have probably saved her life."

"Only half. You found a safe house for her until we can find something better. You are sure this . . . this . . . what is he?"

"A *forçado*," she replied. "He is a Portuguese bullfighter. He will care well for her in his house. He is a good man."

"And brave," Carter said. "If they link him to Fernando, he's liable to have trouble."

"He can handle trouble," Leonita said with a smile. "A *forçado* is a man who, when he fights the bull, does so with his bare hands."

Carter nodded, watching the white-clad figure turn a curve in the road and disappear. He'd seen the way the Portuguese bullfighters threw their bodies over the horns of the bull and wrestle them to a standstill, while another crazy one grabbed the bull's tail to belittle the beast.

"And this *forçado*," Carter asked, starting the car, "he's a good friend of Fernando?"

"Oh, yes. He is a brother of Fernando's mistress."

Carter could only shake his head as he eased out the clutch.

Just one big happy family, he thought.

SEVEN

At one time the O Vapor had been a passenger steamer that plied its way between Lisbon and Barreiros across the Tagus River. Now it was moored in the elegance of the Vilamoura marina, and its polished brass fittings, varnished wood panels, and deeply upholstered velvet chairs were all accouterments for a restaurant of distinction.

Starting his drunk act again, Carter weaved the Cortina a bit as he came down off the cliff toward the ocean.

Off to their left gleamed the huge Vilamoura hotel, and beyond the buildings was the muted green of the hotel's two golf courses. Directly below them, lights strung on poles around its complete perimeter, was the marina with over a hundred luxury boats of all shapes and sizes bobbing at pier or anchor.

"That's him in the Fiesta," Carter growled, braking erratically into the parking lot. "Don't look . . . except in your rearview mirror."

Leonita took a quick glance and shook her head negatively in Carter's direction. "I don't know him. In fact, I've never seen him before."

"I guessed as much. Two-to-one he's imported."

Carter parked the car and did the number again on Leonita's shoulder all the way around the marina to where the O Vapor was moored.

"She must have been quite a gal in her day," he said as they moved up the gangway.

"Yes. A bygone, romantic day, when . . ."

He could feel a slight stiffness in her shoulders, and out of the corner of his eye caught her chewing on her lower lip.

"A bygone day," he said, "when there wasn't such a great need for a man like me."

"I didn't mean that."

"But you thought it," he replied.

"Yes. But I also thought of a bygone day when we would have sailed this ship to Barreiros on a moonlit night, held hands on the bow over Cointreau, and then went below to make love with the rocking waves."

Carter stopped and gently tugged her into the shadows. He tilted her face up to his and pressed his lips over hers. Her body, like a dry well suddenly filling from an underground spring, swelled against him.

"You do your part," he whispered, "and I'll do mine. And when this is over I promise you a holiday of romance like you've never had."

Lightly her right index finger sealed his lips.

"Never promise what only God can grant. Shall we go?"

Carter nodded, and together they moved back into the lights.

"Did you call?"

"Yes, from the *taberna*. They would be only too happy to have Leonita Silva sing the fado at O Vapor tonight . . . especially for free!"

"Good!" Carter suddenly roared in a loud voice. "Now, c'mon, let's take a turn around this old tub before we go in!"

They made two turns until Carter had the complete lay of the land—or, in this case, the boat and sea.

"I can take off from here," he said, pausing on the shadowed port side. "I can stash my clothes there, behind those pipes."

Leonita rolled her eyes to the slips between the O Vapor and the end of the marina, and then on into the blackness of the ocean.

"It is a long swim," she whispered, squeezing his arm.

"It is. But look there."

"A life preserver?"

Carter nodded, smiling. "I'll have it back before they miss it."

"Let us hope so."

The maître d' was all charm and bowing effusiveness as he led them to a table and brought wine. Only Carter's drooping eyelids and slouched figure made them out to be less than royalty to the people seated around them.

"Get a table in the back," Carter whispered. "Tell him I have to pee a lot."

Leonita requested and it was granted, at once.

Carter lit a cigarette and checked his watch.

It was ten o'clock sharp.

The big black with the pink scar came in just after Leonita had started to sing. From a slouching position deep down in the red velvet chair, Carter popped him a quick look now and then through hooded, somnambular eyes.

From the bored expression on his face it was clear to Carter that the man was not a connoisseur of the fado.

Good, he thought, *another point in our favor*!

Since they had been seated, Carter had gone to the men's room four times—two since Pink Scar's arrival. Each of those times the man was tense until he again saw Carter slumped in his chair.

Now Carter checked his watch and headed for yet another pit stop.

This time the man barely noticed his departure.

Carter killed nearly five minutes in the john and then returned to his table. Again there was only a cursory glance from the watchdog.

"More wine, *senhor?*"

"Yeah, yeah," Carter growled, "more wine."

The waiter arrived with more wine just as the audience erupted with applause and loud calls for yet another song from Leonita.

The combination of Carter's drugged posture, the fact that he had ordered yet another carafe of wine, and having to sit through another round of fado, worked.

The broad-shouldered African dropped some escudo notes on the bar and, with a look on his face that Carter read as disgust, fled the room.

Ah, the saints are with us! Carter mused to himself, letting his eyes float from the door to the hauntingly beautiful face of Leonita in the spotlight.

She was singing full out now, holding the entire room spellbound with her voice and the mood of the song.

But somehow, even in the light's harsh glare, her eyes found Carter's. They riveted on him, saying the language of the song, and yet much more.

Gently Carter placed the tips of three fingers of his right hand to his lips and then blew her a kiss. He was sure that the nod she gave him in reply had been perceptible only to him.

He slipped from the chair and moved toward the rest rooms in the rear. Only this time he didn't stop, but went on down the passageway and through a hatch to the port side aft deck.

In two leaps he was up a ladder to the 'A' deck and scanning the pier leading back along the marina.

There were several people strolling back and forth, talking, hand-holding, or just ooing and ahhing the pleasure craft.

But there was no broad-shouldered black with a pink scar on his cheek and a bulge under his left armpit.

In no time Carter was back down on 'B' deck and all the way aft on the port side where it was almost total darkness.

In quick, sure, deft movements he removed Wilhelmina's shoulder rig and did a few strap adjustments until it became an old-style Western hip holster. Then he stripped: coat, tie, shirt, pants, shoes and socks, right down to a tight-fitting tank suit.

He rolled clothes and shoes into a bundle, secured them with his belt, and then stashed them behind the port side vent piping. After making sure that there were no telltale signs sticking out, he transferred Hugo's spring sheath to his leg and strapped Wilhelmina on his hip.

Carefully he went over the watertight oilskin he had wrapped around the Luger earlier. Satisfied, he made his way to the rail and stepped over.

The last thing he did before dropping silently into the water was to detach one of the life preservers that ringed the rail every ten feet around the O Vapor.

For ten seconds the water on his body was like being submerged in a bucket of ice. Carter remained still for a full two minutes, letting the shock wear away. Several times he dipped his head in the water to get used to it. The frigid water was also an excellent antidote for the alcohol he'd consumed that evening.

When his body was fully acclimated and his mind was clear, he set off, riding the life preserver, kicking with his feet.

He moved along the port side of the O Vapor and then under the pier. There he used the mooring lines of each docked boat to pull him toward the mouth of the marina and save his strength for the sea swim ahead.

At the outward end of the pier he paused. Beneath the water he could feel the ebb and flow of the tide. In the sky there was a quarter moon, its brightness mottled by gray clouds scudding across its surface.

Carter shook his head and smiled.

Now, he thought, *if all this luck only holds.*

With a powerful kick he pushed off one of the pier ties and began kicking straight out to sea. He knew Fernando's small boat would be without running lights, so he kept swiveling his head back to the marina for sightings. When he was far enough out, he veered over into a direct line with the center of the marina's mouth and headed out again.

In his mind, Carter counted off yards. When he was pretty sure he had passed fifty, he slowed his pace and swiveled in the water a full 360 degrees.

To his right, about twenty yards away, he made the vague outline of a small boat's fantail gently rolling with the incoming tide.

As silently as possible he made for it, flipping his mind back over what Fernando had told him: "My boat is called *The Shadow*."

Three yards away, Carter dived and came up near the bow on the starboard side. There, in red paint and flowing script, was *O Sombra*.

"Fernando!" Carter hissed.

"Boa noite, senhor."

Carter whirled. Fernando was not more than a foot behind him, the top of his powerful shoulders clad in a wet suit. His wide face was split in a toothy grin.

Carter returned it. He was pleased. The guy had heard Carter in the water and slipped into the sea himself until a positive ID could be made.

Carter hadn't seen or heard him.

"Good evening yourself, *mon ami*."

"Shall we go aboard?" Fernando replied, slipping an ugly-looking skinning knife between his teeth and hoisting himself over the boat's gunwale.

Carter followed, and gratefully accepted the wet suit Fernando offered. As he pulled the rubber skin over his own flesh, the big Portuguese rigged sail. In no time they were skimming west, riding the half-cresting waves.

"How long to the point?"

"Fifteen, maybe twenty minutes. I'll stay out until we are beyond Paragem's villa, then ride the tide straight in."

Carter nodded and hunkered down in the bow, wishing he had a cigarette. His ears filtered the sounds that floated over the water. None resembled the sound of a powerboat engine.

The minutes dragged by, and then, squinting his eyes toward shore, Carter could make out a large white bulk that reflected what little moonlight there was.

"Paragem's yacht?"

"*Oui.*"

The white blur had barely disappeared behind an outcropping of stone when Fernando swung the rudder and the boat heeled over.

"Watch your head, *mon ami.*"

Carter ducked as the boom swung over, barely missing his skull by an inch.

"Thanks," Carter chuckled. "I'm usually a better sailor . . . wasn't paying attention."

"Tricky here," Fernando whispered. "A lot of sandbars, rocks."

Carter felt the boat beneath him move in a zigzag pattern. He could see no more than the giant cliffs growing in size before him. How Fernando could see rocks or sense sandbars in the blackness was a mystery to Carter.

Suddenly the bow lifted and he heard the rasping sound of wood sliding over sand.

"Sandbar?"

"No," Fernando chuckled, "beach."

"Jesus."

"Give me a hand!"

Fernando was already over the side, knee-deep in the surf, tugging the boat's bow farther up the sandy incline. Carter went over the opposite side and groped for a hold as he listened to Fernando's whispered cadence.

"One . . . two . . . three . . . heave! One . . . two . . . three . . . heave!"

Together they heaved and grunted until a third of the boat was on the beach. Then Fernando ran a bowline up and tied it off around a shaft of jagged rock.

"This way!"

Carter padded down the beach behind him for about twenty yards. Fernando stopped so abruptly that Carter nearly crashed into his looming bulk.

"We go straight out here for about fifteen meters," Fernando said, gesturing in the dim moonlight. "Then we circle around this point like an arc. Be very careful, *mon ami*. The tide is coming in with strength, and the rocks just below the surface and around us will be very sharp. It will skin you like a knife."

For the second time that night Carter silently thanked the other man for the wet suit he wore. If the tide did wash him against the rocks, at least the rubber outer skin would take most of the punishment.

"What about the other side of the point?" Carter asked, noticing for the first time a half-chewed cigar protruding from the corner of Fernando's mouth.

"A small cove, maybe twenty meters wide. It can be very dangerous when the tide comes in, because a cave extends just at the water line that goes deep into the bowels of the earth."

"And if you hit it just right, with the tide taking you in, it could sweep you down?"

"Exactly," Fernando said. "But the tide should be above the top of the cave opening by now."

Carefully Fernando took the ragged cigar and, as if it were gold, placed it on a nearby rock.

"To remind me to return," he said with a chuckle. "We go!"

He plunged into the frothing water with Carter close behind. Both were powerful swimmers, even against the inrushing tide. In no time they had gone beyond the point and made the turn into the arc. When they were around, Carter could feel the increase of tidal pressure against his body.

"Keep swimming out!" Fernando yelled.

Carter nodded his understanding and turned his head toward the sea.

By taking two strong breaststrokes and then easing off, the tide took them in at a slow pace. If they had gone in with it full tilt, there was a better than even chance that a few bones would be broken when the tide slammed them against the side of the cliff.

As it was, Carter felt a jarring jolt against the soles of his feet when they found the cliff. It sent a rocket of pain up the back of his legs and through his spine, but it did no damage.

"Are you all right, *mon ami*?"

"Not too much the worse for wear," Carter replied. "I'll start on this side."

Fernando nodded and swam away into the darkness on the opposite side of the cove.

Carter found the juncture point between the cliff face and the outcropping, and began sliding his hands over the area a few square feet at a time. He worked a yard above the waterline and then dived beneath the surface to do the same there.

It was on his third trip down and toward the center when his hands felt the unmistakable crevices. Because most of them had been made by natural erosion, they weren't spaced in a direct line upward.

But they were there, and they went up.

Carter was completely clear of the water and clinging to the side of the cliff like a leech when he was sure enough to call out.

"Fernando . . ."

"*Oui?*"

"I found them!"

The words were barely out of Carter's mouth when he felt the other man's hand on his ankle.

"Once you are in the cave, *mon ami*, be careful. There may be blowholes in the floor."

"Right."

"Here is a penlight. Shield its light from the opening as much as possible. A light can be seen for miles at sea."

"I know," Carter said, snaking his hand down until his fingers wound around the light.

He rolled it under the waistband of the wet suit and started up.

It was arduous going and hard on the fingers and toes. Twice he tried to pull on a false crevice, only to come away with crumbled limestone and nearly fall.

Finally he was reaching and finding only air.

The mouth of the cave was only about three feet high, but it ran twelve feet across.

"I'm there!" he called, hoping that his voice would only carry to Fernando.

"Good luck, *mon ami*!" came the reply.

Carter heaved himself up and over the rim. Just inside, he lay flat with his body toward the sea and switched on the light. In its narrow beam he saw a coil of wire. Attached to one end was a large, bare bulb. The other end led to a small, one-horsepower gasoline generator.

Carefully he played the light farther back.

Barely a yard inside the opening, the walls and ceiling branched out to form a room eight by eight and almost high enough to stand. The floor was solid beneath a fine powder of limestone dust.

Carter stood and moved inward.

In no time he found the crawl hole Ines had described. One arc of the light told him it was about ten feet long and just big enough for a normal man to get through.

Fernando would never have made it.

He scraped his knees badly twice and made a small tear in one elbow of the suit, but was finally able to drop to the floor of the second room.

It was much larger than the first, and the floor showed debris much the same as humans leave behind them the world over. There were empty food containers, cigarette butts, and wine bottles as well as crushed beer cans in every corner.

Ines hadn't been exaggerating about the many "little

picnics'' she and Jorge had enjoyed in the cave.

Near one wall there was even a rolled-up blanket.

Carter played the light far to the room's back wall until the wall gave way to what appeared to be another tunnel. On closer inspection, he saw that it was a blowhole between the upper and lower cave.

Thrusting his head through it, he could hear water rushing far below.

Turning over, he played the light beam along the upper ridge of the hole. Then he followed it with his hand.

Sure enough, there was a ridge running all along the top of the hole, about eight inches wide.

''Be there, baby, be there!''

It was, right at the top.

Carter pulled it down and slid back into the room.

It was an oilskin-wrapped package about six inches square.

He was tempted to pierce the wrapper just to be sure, but vetoed the thought.

How many oilskin-wrapped packages could there be on rock shelves over blowholes in caves fifty feet above the sea in the Algarve?

Carter was more careful going back through the narrow tunnel, and he suffered no abrasions. At the cave mouth he slithered out until just a portion of his butt still rested on rock, with his legs hanging down.

''Are you there, *mon ami*?''

''*Oui.*''

''I have it,'' Carter said.

''Good . . . get ready!''

Carter raised the package in both hands over his head and riveted his eyes on the darkness far below.

There was a millisecond of light from Fernando's penlight, and Carter lofted the package as accurately as possible toward it.

The splash echoed up to his ears and was quickly followed by more splashing from Fernando's big body.

"I have it. Ready yourself!"

"Ready!"

There was another flash, and Carter hurtled himself out from the wall. He kept his shoulders straight, his head up, and his eyes somewhere out to sea.

The hit was perfect, and seconds later he was surfacing, shaking water from his eyes to stare into Fernando's grinning face.

"We are a fine team, *mon ami*."

"That we are," Carter replied. "Now let's get the hell out of here!"

The sail back to Vilamoura was routine and uneventful.

"You know what to do with it, Fernando," Carter said, perched now on the boat's gunwale and clad again in only the skimpy tank suit.

"*Oui*. Have no fear, it will be waiting for you."

"Good enough. *Adeus!*"

"*Adeus.*"

Carter rolled from the boat into the sea, and Fernando tossed him the life preserver.

Carter had barely started kicking his way back toward the marina when Fernando turned with the wind and *O Sombra* was heading toward Faro.

The swim to the marina was twice as easy and three times as fast as it had been going out. In less than twenty minutes from the time he left Fernando, he was lighting a cigarette and strolling back into the O Vapor dining room.

There were few diners now, but still a lot of drinkers. A jazz trio was on the stage, and a fat German was drunkenly singing drinking songs in a loud bass.

Leonita was calmly sitting at the table, sipping sangria.

"Sorry I was so long, darling," Carter said, sliding into the chair opposite her. "Bit of an upset tummy."

"Is everything all right now?"

"Everything is fine."

"Then, darling," she replied, a little acid in her voice, "I suggest we go. This man is driving me mad."

Carter paid the bill and, as they approached the car, handed her the keys. "You drive."

"Tired?"

"That, and hung over," he replied with a grin. "Remember?"

"Of course. That's why you had to put your head under the faucet in the rest room."

"That's right, darling."

Pink Scar was right behind them all the way to Vale do Lobo. Carter could almost tell from the careless way the man tailed them that he considered the entire evening a waste of time.

Considerably more sober now, Carter approached the night concierge in the hotel.

"I suppose the snack bar is closed?"

"*Sim, senhor*. I am sorry."

"Is there any place I can order some food sent up to the room?"

"There is a small place near the beach, *senhor*, O Caracole. They stay open sometimes until three this time of the year. But they only have fish sandwiches."

"Sounds delicious. Order us up a dozen," Carter said, dropping a few bills on the desk and guiding Leonita by the elbow toward the elevator.

In the room, Carter stripped off his shirt, and Leonita applied medication to the cuts he had suffered from the rocks.

"I was worried about you."

"So was I," he said, sipping from a goblet of brandy. "But Fernando was fantastic."

"I told you he was."

"You should have stayed married . . . I mean, together."

"You are not one to talk," she replied, applying the

burning liquid to a cut with laughing vengeance. "Besides, Fernando is happy with his Camilla, and I have my fado."

Carter was about to reply when a knock on the door sent him lurching from the chair.

"Your sandwiches, *senhor*."

She was a girl of about twenty, with huge, lustrous eyes.

"*Obrigado*," Carter said, taking the package from her hands.

"*Não tem de quê* . . . you . . . are . . . very . . . welcome," she replied, then darted down the hall.

Carter closed the door and turned to face Leonita. "I can see why Fernando is very happy with his Camilla. She is lovely."

"Yes," Leonita said with a shrug. "But very young."

Carter roared with laughter as he upended the box. Sandwiches poured over the coffee table, and there, on top of them, was the oilskin-wrapped package of heroin.

EIGHT

Carter's eyes felt as if they were filled with sand from the Algarve beaches the following morning when the wake-up call came from the desk. Rubbing them with the knuckles of his index fingers only made them more grainy as he rolled from the bed.

He yanked on the cord that opened the bedroom drapes. Even the faint gray light of early dawn seemed to tear at his pupils. With a groan he longingly looked back at the bed, then clawed for a cigarette from the half-crumpled pack on the bedside table.

When he had it going good, he moved to the other bed.

"Hey . . ."

No answer, not even a twitch of movement from the lump under the sheet.

"Up, up, and away, my little Portuguese nightingale!"

Still no sound or movement.

Carter rapped the arch of a softly fleshed thigh with the flat of his hand.

"Go to hell!" came the muffled oath.

"Arise, woman, we only have an hour."

"Already? It is the middle of the night!"

"Nay, dawn breaks over yonder sea," he announced, bringing her upright with another sharp rap on the rump. "Ring for breakfast while I shower."

"So you can eat while I shower?"

"Something like that."

A pillow hit him in the back as he disappeared through the bathroom door.

As the alternating cold and hot water of the shower pelted him into wakefulness, Carter went over the new day.

Even though he had been weary the preceding night after the package had arrived, he had made the obligatory call to Dupont Circle in Washington. Because it wasn't a scrambled call, he and Hawk had talked in well-worn riddles.

But Carter managed to convey to the head of AXE the importance of the "item" he had acquired.

In turn, Hawk conveyed the message that there was too much information from his end for the current call. It would be best if Carter took a little trip the following morning, north.

So, as much as he hated to leave the Algarve even for one day, and particularly when the situation was just starting to heat up, Carter would be on the 7:30 A.M. Air Portugal flight from Faro to Lisbon.

"Are you about through?"

"I am through," Carter replied, walking into the bedroom with a towel draped around his middle.

She passed him stark naked, a cup of coffee in one hand and a Danish in the other.

"*Bom dia*, Senhor Carter."

"*Bom dia*, Menina Silva."

He watched her dancing buttocks until they disappeared into the bathroom.

God, he thought, *how domestic we've become!*

They checked out, and Carter himself carried the bags into the parking lot.

"See him?" he asked, crawling in behind the wheel.

"*Sim,*" she said with a nod.

Pink Scar's daytime replacement lounged against the

same Fiesta, reading a newspaper. He was young and quite tall, but not reed-thin, with a solidly built torso like an acrobat. Huge, goggle-type sunglasses almost obscured the upper part of his face, and a flowing mustache did its best to cover the lower part. Despite his youth, his black, wavy hair was thin and already working its way up his forehead.

"Not very smart of them to use the same car, is it?" Leonita asked as Carter wheeled the Cortina from the parking lot.

He smiled and patted her knee. "You're catching on very fast."

On the road to Faro and the airport, Carter made no effort to lose the Fiesta. Quite the opposite, in fact. He slowed at caution lights until they turned red so that the other driver would have no trouble keeping pace with them.

By the time he had parked the Cortina at the airport, Carter had filled Leonita in on his plan of attack, or, in this case, departure.

In the terminal he checked in the Cortina, at the same time reserving another car for Leonita's use. He chose a Fiesta and flashed a tongue-in-cheek grin at her as he did so.

"And when will you be wanting the Fiesta, sir? On your return?" the rental car clerk asked.

"No, in about forty-five minutes."

The clerk shrugged. "Americans."

From the rental car counter they crossed the terminal to Air Portugal's domestic ticket sales, where Carter purchased two Lisbon tickets, a one-way and a round-trip. When he had tickets, boarding passes, and seat assignments, he returned to Leonita.

"Coffee?"

"That is the plan," she replied with a grin.

The terminal coffee shop was small, like the minuscule cups they used to serve the thick, bitter liquid. But then the cups had to be small. Few people could digest more than three swallows of the coffee in one sitting.

"Is he here?" Carter whispered.

"Yes. He is sitting there by the door, in the red shirt and black pants."

Carter carelessly glanced up.

The man was short but built like a bull, with powerful shoulders and thick arms. Beneath the table Carter could see sinewy, corded thighs in the tight pants ripple each time he moved. His eyes darted once in their direction, and Carter thought he saw in them calculated amusement.

Carter wondered if that was the way he looked at the bull before he dared the beast to try his best to gore him.

"He looks like a *forçado*," Carter growled around his coffee cup. "I have no doubt he could wrestle bulls with his bare hands!"

As they exited, Leonita gave the *forçado*—the brother of her husband's mistress—a short nod. He replied with just a blink of his eyes and a tiny curl of his lips.

It was a strange world.

"Take a seat in the waiting area," Carter said when they were back in the terminal proper. "I'll make my call."

She nodded and turned away.

Carter found a bank of telephones and fished the piece of paper from his wallet that José Paragem had given him. When he had deciphered the scrawled number, he dropped a coin in the slot and waited through the rings.

"*Está.*"

Carter was surprised that Paragem himself answered the phone, especially at this hour. The man definitely appeared to Carter to be a night person.

"Paragem, this is Carter."

"Thank God you have called!"

"Oh? Something the matter?"

Carter knew damn well something was the matter. Even

if he hadn't known of Ines's disappearance, it was obvious from Paragem's raspy voice.

"There has been a complication," came the reply. "You will have only one run to get the information you need."

"What kind of complication?"

"A . . . personal matter."

"I don't know if we can hit the right boat to find the warehouse or shipping point in just one run."

"Damnit, you will have to!"

Paragem's voice had now gone up a full octave to almost a state of shrillness. Carter could almost see the sweat dripping from the man's fat chin.

"If we have to, we have to," Carter replied. "When?"

"Tomorrow night."

"No way."

"It is the only way, Carter. I must be out of Portugal the following day."

"Your personal problem must be a big one," Carter said dryly, "but I'll see what I can do. I'm on my way to Lisbon now to see about your request."

There was an audible sigh of relief from the other end of the line.

"The envelopes have already been delivered. If it is 'go' tomorrow night—which I am sure it will be—the signal will go out at about eight o'clock."

"I'll try to have my people ready."

"You *must* have your people ready," he hissed.

"I'll bring the papers back with me from Lisbon."

"Good. There is one other thing . . ."

"Yes?"

There was a long, dead silence, as if Paragem were weighing his next words very carefully.

"Are you still there?" Carter asked at last.

"Yes, yes. I am trying to think of the American expression for treachery."

"Try double cross."

"Yes, double cross. Do not double-cross me, Carter. I can be a very dangerous man when I am backed into a corner."

"Yeah, I imagine. Like a rat."

"Humorous, very humorous. The girl . . . Ines?"

"What about her?"

"She has disappeared."

"So what? When I saw her by the pool she looked like just a piece of fleshy fluff you kept around the house."

"In many ways she was. She delivered some of the envelopes for me, but other than that, she knew very little."

"So, what's the problem?"

"Nikko has discovered that Jorge Silva was the girl's lover. As such, she might know where the merchandise we mentioned is hidden. My employer has given me forty-eight hours to find the girl and the merchandise. Now you can see why I must get out of Portugal quickly."

"I assume you're telling me all this for a reason."

"The girl was gone right after your visit. You cannot blame me, Carter, for wondering."

"Paragem, I hardly looked at her above the bikini top. I couldn't tell you what she even looked like."

"Very well. It's just . . . well, she has, shall we say, strayed before. But I have always found her in a few hours. This time, though, she's gone without a trace. You can hardly blame me for wondering if she didn't have help."

"Use your head, Paragem. It would be pretty hard for an American in Portugal, moving around like I have been, to hide a young Portuguese girl."

"Yes, I suppose so, but you can see the problem. Call me when you return from Lisbon. I will set a pickup for the papers."

"Will do."

Carter broke the connection and stood for a full minute, staring at his hand on the instrument.

Once again, those few kilos of opium or refined heroin had taken on a consequence and importance that seemed all out of proportion.

A few kilos out of twenty or more being imported twice or more a month.

It didn't fit.

What was so goddamned important about those particular kilos that would make *the man* come down so hard on Paragem, a vital link in his smuggling chain?

And then an odd question struck him: Did the fact that Coco Chanette accompanied that particular shipment have some significance?

Had it been only coincidence that Alvarez had been aboard the boat that night instead of a planned meeting, as Carter had originally thought?

Or had a meeting been planned and had Chanette used it for a dual purpose—to waste Alvarez *and* personally deliver one of the special shipments?

Nick Carter meant to find out.

He rescued a second coin from his pocket, dropped it in the slot, and this time dialed from memory.

"*Sim?*"

"Fernando?"

"*Oui.* You are at the airport?"

"Yes, everything's moving. How are you coming with the list?"

"I have spotted eight of them. I should know the remaining two by this evening."

"Good. How about the radio?"

"It will be installed by noon."

"Will be in touch."

"*Adeus.*"

"*Au revoir,*" Carter replied and hung up.

Halfway to the Air Portugal waiting area, Carter spotted the day watch carefully reading the hotel advertisements strung along the terminal wall. He wasn't obvious, but then he didn't have to be. He was a foot taller than everyone around him.

Paragem, Carter thought, would really sweat it when he got the report from this one and Pink Scar that ol' Nick Carter had no contact with little Ines. The fat man obviously didn't have any place else to look for his flown bird.

Carter was only hoping that Paragem's new fear would work in his favor, and for a long enough period of time.

"Everything all right?" Leonita asked as Carter slid into the vinyl couch beside her.

"Peachy keen," he replied, checking the wall clock.

It was seven o'clock. The ETD on the Lisbon flight was seven-thirty.

"*Que significa* 'peachy keen'?" she asked, frowning.

"Another American slang term, meaning all the windmills are turning fine."

They called the flight for boarding at seven-ten.

"Time to go," Carter said.

"Yes. Be careful."

"You be careful," he replied.

Leonita stood and moved through the milling crowd across the tile floor. Carter watched the voluminous white skirt swish around her long, trim legs. Just before she entered the door marked *Senhoras*, she pulled the ever present shawl—this one also stark white and thickly knitted—up over her head.

Oh, yes, Carter thought, *in that outfit she will stand out in any crowd*.

Nothing is quite so sublime as the obvious.

He caught a quick glance of boy watchdog where he still stood by the hotel posters. His high forehead was furrowed quizzically as his eyes darted to the clock, the emptying waiting area, and the rest room door.

Don't worry, my friend, Carter said to himself, *she's not about to miss the flight*.

Lighting a last cigarette, Carter watched the flow of women move out of the rest room. Nearly all of them were dressed head to toe in traditional black, so she was hard to spot.

Carter himself would have missed her had not the beefy bullfighter emerged from behind a nearby pillar and taken her by the elbow.

They were about twenty yards down the concourse toward the exit when a flash of white that stood out in the crowd drew Carter's eye back to the door.

Quickly he crushed out the cigarette, grabbed the bags, and rushed to meet her.

"Leonita . . . Leonita, damnit, hurry, we're about to miss the plane!" he called in a loud, clear voice.

Side by side, with Carter's bulk on her right, between her and High Forehead's line of sight, they moved quickly through the waiting area.

Carter handed over the boarding passes and they were through the gate, moving down the ramp to the plane.

A quick, sideways look told Carter that Paragem's man was lounging indolently against a pillar with his arms folded across his chest.

Just from the look on his face, Carter could tell that he assumed his job was over, at least for a while.

Halfway down the ramp, she tilted her face up toward Carter. There was a broad grin on her crimson lips and even through the dark glasses he could see the twinkle in her eyes.

"*Bom dia*, Senhor Nick."

"*Bom dia*, Ines."

As the plane taxied up to the gate in Lisbon, Carter pressed a thick envelope into Ines's hand and passed her the note Leonita had written for him in Portuguese.

It would have been impossible for him to have told her everything with his limited knowledge of the language.

Ines,

There is a great deal of money in the envelope. Take care of it, and I hope it will make for you a new life.

Don't worry about the amount of money, which I am sure you will think phenomenal. Believe me when I say that I am confident that your help has earned it.

In two days' time, call this number in Lisbon: 411-564. Ask for Bill MacHugh. He will have papers for you, and he will arrange for your transportation out of the country as far as Seville, Spain.

From there you are on your own.

> Boa sorte,
> Senhor Nick

She read the letter slowly and with difficulty, forming the words on her lips. There were tears in her eyes when she turned to look at him.

They made Carter feel good. They were true tears of gratitude.

It was nice for a change.

By the time the crowd had started moving down the aisle, she had carefully stuffed the envelope in her purse.

Carter wondered what she would do with fifteen thousand dollars. He hoped she would use it to never again fall into the clutches of a man like José Paragem.

From Leonita's bag beneath the seat she had already changed clothes in one of the plane's lavatories. She now wore a beige traveling suit, complete with a matching crocheted straw beret that obscured a corner of her face.

It wasn't perfect, but if Paragem or High Forehead at the airport had called ahead to arrange a tail in Lisbon, it was ten-to-one against her being spotted in the new clothes. Particularly if she got off the plane alone, before Carter.

"It's time now," Carter said, gently squeezing her knee. "*Adeus. Foi um grande prazer.*" And, indeed, it had been a great pleasure.

Ines stood, took one step, and then whirled to lean over the seat. She took Carter's face in her hands and then pressed her lips to his in a quick, hard kiss.

"*Adieu, moi grand homme,*" she whispered in incorrect but heartfelt French.

Carter smiled as he watched her walk down the aisle. He felt good.

In fact he felt very good, very much like a "big man."

The plane was nearly empty when Carter himself walked down the aisle and stepped through the hatch.

It wasn't too hard to pick out Bill MacHugh where he stood waiting in the middle of the concourse.

His hair, years before, had been a thick, reddish mane. Now he was balding, and what was left was turning silver with just a suggestion of the reddish tint left. The paunch that hung over his belt was one third good food and two thirds beer and good Irish whiskey.

MacHugh had always drunk a lot, even in the line of duty, but it had never stopped him from doing that duty.

"Nick, it's been a long time. Sorry I wasn't in Lisbon to greet you a few days ago when you were first here."

Despite the sagging frame in the equally sagging suit, MacHugh's grip when he shook Carter's hand was like a vise.

"Mac, how have you been?"

"Bit of an ulcer, a migraine now and then, sore joints, and I can't seem to get it up too often anymore, but other than that I'm chipper."

The grin on his florid face was a yard wide, and Carter matched it.

"I didn't need you before, here in Lisbon, but I think I can use you now."

"Good enough. Come along, I've a car waiting."

Driving into Lisbon proper from the airport, Carter

filled MacHugh in on everything that had occurred the last few days.

"What do you make of the 'special' heroin?"

"Don't know," Carter replied. "That's why I want it analyzed. Can you get it done?"

"Not here," MacHugh said. "I'll have to get it over to our people in Madrid. As you know, it's a one-man show for us here in Lisbon. Not like the old days during the cold war. Lisboa was a spy's paradise then!"

"Can you pouch it over . . . through the embassy here?" Carter asked. "I don't have enough time to do it the usual way."

The 'usual way' was an intracountry smuggling run. That would take days to set up.

"Oh, yes," MacHugh said in response to Carter's query. "Chaps at State don't like us much, but they'll give me a courier run to Madrid if I ask for it."

"Has Hawk called?"

MacHugh nodded. "This morning. Gave me a lot, and gave me a call time in case you want to clarify back with him."

"Good. There's another matter I'd like you to set up for me: a girl."

Carter explained about Ines and what he wanted MacHugh to produce for her.

"Simple," the man said. "Got that kind of stuff on file. Here we are."

It was a bright new building in the newer section of Lisbon. The Amalgamated office on the fifth floor was also bright and new, but it was a mess.

"Sorry about this."

"Never mind," Carter said with a laugh. "I've worked with you before . . . remember?"

From a wall safe MacHugh produced the safe phone, a sheaf of papers, and a fifth of Irish whiskey.

"Join me?"

"No, thanks," Carter replied. "It's a little early and

I've got to keep a clear head . . . for a while."

"Ah, you young ones," MacHugh said, rolling his expressive eyes into his head and retreating to the outer office. "I'll whip up an escape plan for your teen-age Mata Hari."

"You do that," Carter said, his mind already on the matter at hand.

For the next two hours Carter pored over the life of Ramon Alvarez.

As a young officer he had been exemplary, mostly in lower-echelon intelligence work and later, as he slowly rose in the ranks, as a troubleshooter for military intelligence units around the world.

It had been only in the last couple of years that his career seemed to be in limbo. Because of so much undercover work, the man's marriage was in trouble. Also during that time, there were some vast discrepancies in agency money use. It had never been proven that any money dispersed to him for agency use in the field had found its way back into Alvarez's own pocket, but there was reason for suspicion.

That alone meant little. Hadn't Carter himself just bent the rules fifteen thousand dollars' worth?

But the cases were obviously different.

According to the most recent interview with the commander's widow, Roberta Alvarez, her husband had been in constant money trouble in the months before his death.

She had stated that her husband had also become increasingly bitter over being passed over for promotion. He had already made plans to resign his commission and had made several business investments to prepare for that day.

There was one big problem: Ramon Alvarez was a poor businessman and an even worse speculator.

Just prior to his requesting and obtaining this recent NATO undercover assignment in Portugal, all his business deals had gone sour.

All in all, the file gave Carter little to go on. It did little more than confirm the reasons for the man's turning: he was broke, getting broker, and feeling that life and the military had given him a raw deal.

The last part of the file contained a transcript of the interview with Roberta Alvarez and a list of names.

The names were Alvarez's Washington friends, acquaintances, and former coworkers. There was a thumbnail sketch of each one, and also their present occupations and whereabouts.

The friends were few and the acquaintances were inconsequential, beyond telling Carter that they were probably another reason for the breakup of the man's marriage.

Nearly all of them were women: female bartenders, B-girls, secretaries, and a few hairdressers.

Ramon Alvarez obviously loved ladies . . . lots of them.

Only one name popped up off the list to send a prickle up Carter's spine: Brigadier General Jeremy S. Craylon.

Like Alvarez, General Craylon had been in military intelligence. The dates of his tour in Washington fit Ramon Alvarez's almost to the day. He had also been burned out doing undercover work and was eventually reassigned.

His assignment? . . . head of purchasing for all the officer and NCO clubs in Europe.

Carter practically dived for the safe phone. It was a half hour before the designated call time Hawk had set to call Washington, but this was too hot to wait.

Bateman caught the urgency in Carter's voice. Even though David Hawk was in a meeting, she put Carter through.

"You're a half hour early, N3," Hawk rasped without bothering with a hello.

"I know that, sir, but there's one name on this list you sent MacHugh—"

"Brigadier General Jeremy S. Craylon."

"Yes," Carter said, a bit of the wind easing from his sails.

"He's been checked out, Nick," came the reply. "Because of his job in Frankfurt he was obviously number one on my list. His reputation is spotless, as is his character, his bank accounts, everything. There's no way."

"Nevertheless, I'd like to get to him. Can you set it up?"

"One minute . . ."

While he was on hold, Carter yelled to MacHugh in the other room.

"Mac?"

"Yo?"

"Got any coffee around here?"

MacHugh scrounged until he found an almost clean cup and poured Carter a cup from a pot sitting on a hot plate.

"N3?"

"I'm here."

"You've got it. Use your press card from Amalgamated as cover to interview him. We'll play it for *Stars and Stripes*, and tell him it goes on the wire if it's interesting enough. Pick a subject."

"Entertainment for the troops in Europe?"

"Good enough, but it will have to wait."

"Wait?" Carter repeated, doing his very best to keep the frustration out of his voice.

"Until we find him. He's on leave with his wife and children. They're bicycling across Europe, and his office only knows part of his itinerary."

"Jesus, what happens if the Russians launch?"

"They won't be aiming for the service clubs," Hawk replied with a chuckle.

"Okay, let me know through Mac as soon as Craylan is located."

"Will do. One more thing, N3."

"Yes?"

"Our people in Algiers report a lot of odd activity surrounding that end of the operation and the Chanette woman."

"What kind of activity, and why odd?"

"It looks like they're closing down."

Carter's knuckles went white on the phone. The run was set for the next night. Could this be the last run, now that they knew that there was a heavyweight in the game?

"Give me the Algiers contact," Carter said. "I think I'm going to want an hourly movement report on Coco Chanette."

Hawk gave him the information. Carter scribbled it down and hung up.

"Mac, can you put an Air Force jet on hold for me for the next seventy-two hours? I might not need it, but if I do I'll need it fast."

"Where to?"

"Don't know yet. AXE Berlin has to locate a bicycling general for me first."

"Have to be pretty high authority."

"It is."

"You got it."

"Also, I need another set of phony papers—passport, birth certificate, the whole works."

"Man or woman."

"Man. His real name is José Paragem. When they're done, send them by courier down to Lagoa in the Algarve. Here's the address. And, Mac. . .?"

"Yeah?"

"Don't make 'em too good, in case he gets away from me."

NINE

The same car rental clerk waited on Carter at the Faro airport.

"Senhor Carter, you already have a Fiesta rented with us."

"I know that."

"And you want *another* car?"

"Yes. We're a two-car family."

Carter pushed his Eurobank card across the counter.

"Amalgamated Press and Wire Services?"

"Yes."

"I will have to check the card, *senhor*."

"You do that."

Five minutes later she was back.

"You have unlimited credit on this card, *senhor*," she said, her eyes wide.

If you only knew, Carter thought.

He picked up the car and stopped at a phone booth just outside the airport parking lot.

Paragem's phone didn't answer. He hung up and dialed again.

"*Está.*"

"Fernando, *por favor.*"

"He is not here."

"Where is he?"

"Who is this?"

"Carter. Is this Camilla?"

"*Sim*. Fernando is with his wife."

There was a great deal of anger in Camilla's voice.

Goddamn, Carter thought, *that's all I need now . . . a family squabble*.

"At a villa on the beach road just east of Carvoeiro. It is near—"

"A church. I know," Carter replied. "If he shows up there before I catch him, tell him to call me."

Silence.

"Camilla . . .?"

"Yes, I will," she said and hung up.

There was no tail from the airport, and he didn't pick up one on the east-to-west highway.

Leonita's Fiesta was parked at the end of the villa's circular drive. There was a gleaming BMW motorcycle just behind it.

Carter grabbed his bag from the car and walked up the road and into an arbor heavy with hibiscus and bougainvillea. The scent almost overpowered him, but not half as much as the sight of Leonita when she opened the door to greet him. She was back in the one-piece white swim suit.

"Hi . . ."

"*Boa noite*," she said, thrusting a scotch into his hand and molding her body to his. The kiss said worlds, and the tongue clawing its way between his lips said more.

"This could grow on a guy," he grinned, catching his breath when she released him at last.

"I hope so. Fernando is by the pool."

"Have you been hanky-pankying while I was at the office?"

"If hanky-panky means what I think it does, you do not mean it," she replied, laughing.

"I don't. I only hope Fernando can convince Camilla of that."

Carter dropped his briefcase on the parquet floor inside the door, and they wound their way through the villa, talking as they walked.

"Did you have any trouble with the villa on such short notice?"

"None. The real estate woman thought I was insane, but I told her it was our honeymoon."

"Wonderful."

"Ah, Nick, *bon soir*!" Fernando roared as they emerged onto the patio. "I thought you would arrive soon, so I waited."

"*Bon soir, mon ami.*"

Carter winced as the big man's paw engulfed and tried to crush his hand.

"The radio is in and tested. Here is the list of boats and their owners."

Carter accepted the paper, scanned it quickly, and stuffed it in his jacket pocket.

"Have they been following you?"

Fernando nodded. "All day, the bandaged one, Nikko. But what can they do?"

"Nothing, I hope. We go tomorrow night as soon as I get the info from Paragem."

"Good. How do you like my machine?"

"The BMW?"

"*Oui*. It will fly!" he said, then split his face with a wide grin. "It is a business expense, yes?"

"Yes," Carter said, matching the other's grin. "Where do we meet tomorrow night?"

"Cape St. Vincent . . . near Belixe. I have shown Leonita the place."

"Good," Carter said and turned to the woman. "Have they spotted you yet?"

"By now, I assume they have," she said and shrugged. "But it is too late. Ines is safe, isn't she?"

"Very," Carter said, and he explained what MacHugh

would be doing for the girl in a couple of days.

Fernando stood. "I must go. Until tomorrow night. Leonita."

"*Adeus*, Fernando."

When the giant was gone, Carter also stood. "I've got to make a call. Fix me another drink and run a tub, will you? I feel like relaxing."

He let Paragem's phone ring ten times, hung up, and dialed again.

Still no answer.

Odd, Carter thought, *the fat man knew, in fact he told me to call when I got back to the Algarve.*

"Nick?"

"Yes?"

"The bath is ready . . . up here."

Carter tugged at his clothes, trailing them behind him as he walked across the huge master suite.

"Where are you?"

"In here."

Indeed she was, nakedly golden in an olympic-size tub.

"You said you wanted to relax." She grinned.

"Haven't we done this before?"

"If it was successful the first time, why will it not be again?"

Carter stepped into the tub and eased down. He slid his legs beneath hers and tugged with his hands at her hips.

Leonita practically floated forward until she was on his lap, with her breasts gently nudging his face.

"Nick . . ."

"Leonita . . ."

It was eminently successful the second time.

Carter drove by Paragem's villa twice. He had been calling the man for the last three hours with no results, so now he was checking for himself.

There was a single light on in one wing of the second floor. Other than that, the front was dark. From a rise about a hundred yards down the road, Carter could see the patio area in the rear of the villa. The patio floods were off, but the underwater pool lights were sending an eerie green incandescence up from the water.

Entering the grounds of the villa at this time of night—it was just past one in the morning—might be a foolish move, but Carter felt that something was wrong.

After a wild hour of lovemaking, both in the bath and the bed with Leonita, Carter had napped for an hour. Then he had started calling again.

Now a sense of frustration and urgency filled him.

Had Paragem gotten cold feet after all and skipped?

If that were the case, *how* had he skipped?

The big Mercedes Carter had seen the previous day was in the drive, and the white yacht was still moored at its dock at the foot of the cliff.

Carter made a third pass at the house and pulled into a grove of trees about a hundred yards beyond. A light rain had started, and a gentle breeze from the sea blew it into Carter's face as he stepped from the car.

From somewhere, probably Paragem's villa, a radio played.

Carter stayed in the trees for a few minutes, then sprinted up the road and approached the front of the tall, wrought-iron gates that protected the drive.

Other than the usual night sounds, the beating of the sea against the rocks, and the music from the radio, there was no sound.

To his surprise the gate swung silently inward before a gentle push. Carter slipped through the opening and pawed Wilhelmina from under his arm.

The drive made a long, horseshoe arc up to the house. The center of it was laid out in a formal garden of box-wood hedges and bougainvillea. Levering a shell into the Luger's chamber, Carter disregarded the drive and went toward the front door right through the garden.

He kept darting his eyes to both ends of the house as he

moved in a crouch. He hit the top step of the veranda with his shoulder and rolled to the door.

The door was locked.

Back in a crouch, he sprinted to the gate in the side wall he had used before.

It stood wide open.

Taking a deep breath he dived through, gained his feet, and started running. He used a ledge, a tree, another tree, and then a long hedgerow for cover after he gained the lawn area near the pool and the patio.

He made an arc with Wilhelmina in both hands of the whole area.

Nothing. No one. No sound.

"Smells," he whispered. "Stinks to hell."

With his back to the rear wall of the villa, he side-stepped his way to the rear door he had seen Ines use before.

It, too, stood wide open.

"Now it really smells."

Through the door he rolled from side to side, silently bouncing off the walls of a hallway until he found himself in a kitchen. Then he stood, listening.

The sound of the radio was louder now. It came from one of the upstairs rooms. Carter guessed the room with the light, and he headed out.

A large foyer led off the dining room. All was in darkness, but reflected light from the outside, dim as it was, allowed him to make his way.

Opposite the foyer he saw the outlines of furniture, a stairway, but nothing moving. He hit the stairway with his back against the wall, and started up.

The higher he went, the louder was the sound of the radio and the rain beating down on the roof to roll off the eaves. He was near the top when, from somewhere above him, he heard a door bang.

He stopped instantly, Wilhelmina at the ready.

Then the sound of shuffling feet approached him. It was

as if a step were taken, and then the other leg dragged behind.

Suddenly an apparition appeared, half hanging over the banister above him.

Carter froze, bringing Wilhelmina up in both hands and flipping the safety off at the same time.

A jagged spear of lightning flashed across the window at the end of the upper hallway, illuminating the figure above him.

It was Carlo, and Carter could see what made the dragging and shuffling sounds.

Both his legs were in casts. His arms were thick with bandages. But he still managed to hold a .45 in his hands.

Carter just started to squeeze the trigger when Carlo mumbled indistinctly and pitched headlong down the stairs toward him.

Carter braced himself just in time to catch him and, at the same time, knock the .45 from his hand with Wilhelmina.

He rolled the man over in his arms and looked down into his face. The eyes were lifeless, staring coldly up at Carter from their hollow sockets.

Then Carter's own eyes rolled down to the man's chest, and he saw why. There were two neat small-caliber holes in the general locale of Carlo's heart.

Carter stepped aside and let the man fall. As Carlo continued his roll down the stairs, Carter noticed that his own hands were sticky with blood.

He continued up the stairs, pretty sure that if he found Paragem, the man would be dead.

The light he had seen from outside the villa had come from the master suite. A partially packed bag lay on the bed. Beside it was an open briefcase stuffed with French francs. And on the carpet at the foot of the bed was a 9mm Beretta.

Other than that, the room was empty.

In an adjoining bath, Carter washed Carlo's blood from

his hands, then did a quick run-through of the rest of the house.

Back on the patio, he checked the entire pool area, and paused to light a cigarette and think.

Carlo had obviously bought it with the Beretta. But from whom? And where was Nikko, if Carlo was still around? And, most of all, where was Paragem?

At that point, Carter had no answers. In disgust he rolled the cigarette between his thumb and index finger and flipped it toward the clifftop wall.

It came to rest by the gate that fronted the stairs leading down the cliff's face.

Carter remembered the yacht.

With Wilhelmina again in his hand, he went cautiously down the rain-slick stone steps. He kept his eyes darting from bow to aft and deck to deck on the huge white yacht.

At the bottom of the steps, he called out Paragem's name twice.

There was no answer.

He gained the head of the pier but went no farther.

The answer was on the jagged rocks on the opposite side of the pier.

There, bobbing in the froth of the sea, was José Paragem.

He was lying face-up. His face was now tranquil, almost cherubic, and his arms were outstretched at his sides, as if in supplication.

Carter wondered in supplication to whom, or to what.

There was no need to check the body. Carter could see from where he stood that the back of the man's skull was crushed in.

As he made his way back up the stone steps, Carter wondered if a ballistics test on Paragem's right hand would reveal cordite.

TEN

Carter spent most of the day lounging at the villa. Outside, it alternated between gray overcast and downright rain. The weather reports said more of the same with a chance of some fog.

That was good and bad. The boats they would be trailing would have a difficult time seeing them, but they would also have a hard time keeping a fix on whichever boat they picked to follow. Carter had an ace up his sleeve, however, just in case.

Now, with Paragem dead, they would have an added problem to surmount: which freighter had the goods?

Once in the morning and again in the midafternoon, Leonita went out.

The answer was the same each time she returned.

"They're watching us."

"How many?"

"Six," she replied, "three to a car. One car is by the café at the foot of the road to Carvoeiro. The other is parked at a bait shop and service station near the main highway."

Because of the villa's location—on a jutting cliff above Carvoeiro—they were at the arc of a horseshoe. One way went into the village of Carvoeiro, the other took them out on the main highway.

The only other way to exit—without being seen—was off the cliff and into the sea, a thousand feet down a sheer limestone cliff. Carter had no desire to leave that way.

A quick phone call to Fernando, and they solved the problem of one or both of the cars following Carter that night when he rendezvoused with the *O Sombra*.

"You're full of surprises," Leonita said when Carter finished the call.

"That's how I survive in my strange line of work," he said with a grin.

Around five, Carter himself ventured out. He took the coastal road, then angled inland toward the main Algarve highway.

They were waiting: two half-asleep in the front seat, a third playing watchdog while he sucked on a Coca-Cola in a shaded picnic area beside the station.

Carter halted at the stop sign, and the solo man headed for the car at a leisurely pace.

He waited until the solo man was halfway to the car, then he floored the Fiesta in first, cranked the wheel right, and burned the back tires through all four gears.

In the rearview he saw the man begin to sprint and practically dive into the sedan. In seconds the dust was rising around the other car, and then they hit the asphalt of the highway in hot pursuit.

Carter kept the Fiesta floored for nearly three miles until he topped a rise in the road. The downhill side was long and steep. Just over the crest he geared down and lightly pumped the brake a few times.

He was barely a quarter of the distance down the incline, moving at a snail's pace, when the sedan came over the rise behind him like a bull out of a chute.

In the rearview, Carter saw the other driver wildly fighting the wheel as he applied too much brake. The sedan swerved from side to side like a too-far-gone drunk.

At last, less than thirty feet behind Carter, the driver gave up and let his speed take him on around the Fiesta.

"Touché," Carter said aloud, and lit a cigarette as he settled back in the seat. "And now, gentlemen, we'll have a leisurely ride in the country and then a little shopping trip!"

For the next twelve miles, Carter stayed behind them as if he were the tailer and they the tailee.

At the beach road that led down to Albufeira, Carter honked twice, waved at them, and turned.

He had weaved halfway through the village when they slewed around a corner and caught sight of him.

Aimlessly Carter drove through the town, all the way to the bullring.

There he stopped at a bar, went inside, and ordered a beer. Sitting directly in front of a window, he watched them swelter in the car while he took his time sipping the beer.

He repeated the process two more times while driving back into the center of the village. Once there, he parked at the square and again entered a tavern.

"Telefone?"

"Sim," the bartender nodded, gesturing toward the rear.

Carter found the phone and then dialed the now familiar number.

"Está."

"Camilla?"

"Sim."

"Carter. Are you in better spirits this afternoon?" he asked in French.

"Much, Senhor Carter. Fernando has shown me that jealousy of Leonita is foolish."

"Good," Carter replied, smiling. He could guess just how Fernando had shown her. "Is he ready?"

"Sim . . . ready and waiting."

"He" would be Fernando's hand on the boat, a young and burly Dutchman named Lars. Carter hadn't met him, but Fernando trusted him implicitly and had informed

Carter that Lars's love of money was only second to his loyalty to Fernando.

"Tell Lars it is a blue Fiesta, license number N-O-M-dash-twelve."

"N-O-M-dash-twelve," she repeated.

"It is parked just off the square on the street to the marina."

"*Sim*. He will be waiting."

Carter hung up and went back into the sunlight. He circled the square aimlessly twice, until he had all three of them spotted. One had remained in their sedan. It was parked opposite the square from the Fiesta, near a group of open-air stalls selling souvenirs and other tourist trash.

The other two were on foot, one casually window-shopping directly across the street from Carter and moving along with him. The other one stayed several paces behind Carter. He made no pretense of being a tourist, but kept his eyes on Carter like a hawk.

If they had wanted to make a play for him, Carter figured they would have done it on a lonely stretch of open road. They hadn't, and it didn't look as though they meant to.

Therefore, they were a surveillance-and-report team only.

But nevertheless, Carter stayed near people and moved toward the souvenir stalls.

He browsed for twenty minutes, selecting a multi-colored, gaudy shirt, a broad-brimmed Portuguese version of a cowboy hat, and a lightweight jacket with AL-GARVE emblazoned across the back in gold letters.

With his purchases in his bag, Carter moved across the street to a restaurant.

"*Sim, senhor?*"

"*Uma cerveja, por favor.*"

"*Sim.*"

When the waiter returned, Carter paid him and tipped him the price of the beer. "*Telefone?*"

"Sim, senhor." He pointed to one by the rear door opposite the men's room.

"Obrigado," Carter replied.

He sipped away half the beer and made for the phone.

It took a pocket of change, but at last he reached the international exchange and eventually got the Algiers number Hawk had given him.

"Harry Blount, please."

"This is Harry, Nick. How goes it?"

"Right now I'm playing silly games with three of them who look to be from your side of the pond."

"They probably are," the AXE agent replied. "The shop's closed, and all the birds have flown from this end."

"All . . .?" Carter asked with a frown. "Even the woman?"

"She went last."

Carter felt his body tense as he asked Harry Blount the jackpot question. "Please tell me, Harry, that Mademoiselle Chanette is afraid to fly."

"Indeed she is, my friend, at least this trip. She sailed at noon on a tramp called the *Celestial Light*. It's bound for the Azores and then on to Brazil. It's got Libyan registration, but it's been docked here in Algiers for over two weeks. I'd guess waiting for a cargo one hell of a lot more profitable than dates."

"Perfect," Carter sighed. "You don't know how good that news is. My contact here bought the farm last night."

"Glad to be of help," Blount replied. "If you need some more help, there are four of us here with nothing to do now. We can be in Faro by morning."

Carter thought for a moment. If Coco Chanette had closed up shop in Algiers, this was probably the last shipment. Blount and his men would be of little help across the Mediterranean. They just might come in handy here in Portugal.

"Might not be a bad idea, Harry. Even knowing which

freighter to hit, we're still flying blind. Check into the Hotel Eva. It's clean, quiet, comfortable, and overlooks the yacht harbor."

"Got you."

"I'll call you if we need a strike force."

"Good hunting!"

"Good flying," Carter replied and hung up.

He checked the john, found it empty, and entered.

Carefully he reapplied the broad, lip-covering black mustache and shucked the T-shirt he was wearing.

He buttoned on the gaudy shirt. Over it he pulled the ALGARVE jacket, then set the hat on his head at a rakish angle.

Done, he surveyed himself in the cracked mirror.

"The poorest excuse for a disguise I've ever seen," he said aloud, chuckling.

The alley behind the restaurant ran both ways: back to the square and down to the Hotel Sol e Mar, right on the marina.

Carter chose the street to the hotel and skulked from the alley.

One of the walkers made him before he'd gone ten yards and hightailed it back to his fellows.

Carter could almost hear the exchange:

"The fool has changed clothes . . . a stupid tourist disguise!"

"Where?"

"He is heading toward the hotel. He will probably double back to his car."

Which is exactly what Carter did.

They were sure of him, which was just what Carter wanted them to be. All three of them sat in the sedan, waiting at the head of the street where the Fiesta was parked.

Carter didn't even give them a glance as he unlocked the car and slid into the driver's seat.

"Lars?"

"I am here . . . on the back floorboards."

"I'm Carter."

"Glad to meet you."

"Can you ride all the way to Carvoeiro down there?"

"It's a little cramped, but then I'm a fisherman . . . used to close quarters."

"Then here we go!"

Carter drove fast back to the villa, but not fast enough to lose them. At the turn that led out to the cliffs and the villa, they dropped off to resume their watch at the gas station.

Back at the villa, Carter saw a flash of white on the roof and called up to Leonita.

"Are they there?"

"Yes, both cars . . . same men, same position."

"Good. Let's eat."

The meal was sardines. The way Leonita cooked them, over an open fire on the patio, was world class and proved her background was near the sea.

They ate, and took turns napping and watching from the roof.

Carter had the last watch. When the time neared, he brought the binoculars to his eyes a last time. Through the specially fitted infrared night lenses, he saw that all the pawns were in place.

With a growl of satisfaction, he took the inside stairway down to the villa's living room and surveyed Lars.

In the gaudy shirt, jacket, and silly hat, he was a ringer for the way Carter had looked earlier in the afternoon.

"Can you drive as well as Fernando says?"

"Better," Lars replied with a grin.

"Good. Remember, lead them a merry chase, but don't lose them. We want them to think I'm running around the country, not the sea."

"What about the two watching Fernando?" Leonita asked.

"No problem," Carter said. "They'll see him go out for a night of fishing. Without me on board, they'll think that's all he's up to."

Carter checked his watch and pecked Leonita on the cheek.

"You know what to do." She nodded. "Good, let's go!"

By the time Carter gained the roof, both Fiestas were out the villa's front gate and going their separate ways.

Lars was moving fast, raising a cloud of dust on the road that swirled like a brown cape behind him.

He hit the bottom of the hill full out in fourth and barely braked as he roared through the village. Carter shifted the glasses and saw a black sedan, probably a Mercedes, roar out from behind the café in pursuit.

He continued to watch the two sets of lights head inland toward Lagoa until they were lost in the countryside, and then he raced for the other side of the roof.

Leonita was just turning onto the main highway. She was halfway through the gears when the same sedan that had followed Carter that afternoon took off after her.

Carter checked his watch, waited three full minutes, and then raced down through the villa and out into the rear patio. He yanked open the tool storage shed attached to the pool house and from it wheeled the twin to the black BMW motorcycle that had been parked in the driveway the previous day.

Helmet in place, Carter pressed the starter, and the powerful machine roared into life.

Ten minutes later he was through the village of Carvoeiro and doing sixty on the narrow road toward Lagoa and the main east-west highway. Once there, he barely paused for the stop sign, laid the machine over, and headed west.

Little villages and bigger towns flew past: Portimão, Lagos, and within an hour Vila do Bispo. Here he turned left and covered the final six miles to the sea like the wind.

At Ponta de Sagres, he stopped and consulted the map Leonita had drawn.

Belixe was a resort beach nestled into the cliff's face just beyond Sagres. On the far western end of Belixe there was a dirt trail leading off the road. It was about three fifths of a mile to the cliffs from there.

Carter clicked off her words of instruction in his mind:

"At the very edge of the cliff you will see a goat herder's hut surrounded by a rail fence. Follow the fence around to the back of the hut. There you will find the path down the cliff. Be careful, Nick. It is very steep and the BMW is not a goat."

The rain began again at Belixe, not hard, but steady.

Carter used his lights all the way out to the cliff edge beyond Belixe, then doused them. He left the machine on its kickstand, idling, and reconnoitered on foot until he found the hut.

Everything was as Leonita had said. Minutes later he was through the opening and on the narrow path on the face of the cliff.

He flicked the lights in three dots and three dashes and waited, counting off ten seconds in his mind. When they were over, he repeated the signal.

He was barely finished with the last dash when the signal was repeated from far below.

"Good man, Fernando."

Carter turned the lights on full and lifted the darkened shield of the helmet for clearer vision.

Going down, he left the BMW in low gear and rode the rear wheel brake constantly. Even then he had to slow his pace with the handlebar lever that controlled the front wheel brake.

Halfway down, he hit some loose shale and, for breathless seconds, thought he had lost it. It seemed for a heartbeat that he was suspended, weightless, away from the safety of the cliff.

But a little power and he was back on the path.

Twenty feet from the bottom, Fernando's flash came on, the beam playing back and forth across the sand from the rocks to the boat.

When Carter hit the sand, the beam stayed at the boat, hovering over a two-by-ten ramp that rested one end on the beach, the other on the gunwale.

"*Como está*, Nick?" Fernando called as the BMW passed him.

"*Boa noite*," Carter called back and hit the plank dead center.

He went up, over, and came down on the deck with both wheels, skidding to a stop beside the other motorcycle.

While Carter lashed the machines down, Fernando pried the boat off the beach with the plank Carter had used to board.

"Set?" Fernando cried from the tiller.

"Set," Carter said, moving toward him in a crouch even as the bow bit into the incoming waves.

"Any trouble?"

"None," Carter replied. "You?"

"Just a fisherman trying to make a dishonest dollar," the other man said.

"Did you get the smuggler's helpers?"

Fernando nodded. "They will be waiting for Leonita . . . two Galils with five hundred rounds apiece."

"Fernando, you're a genius."

"Not really, *mon ami*. Money, in the terrible world in which we live, will buy anything."

"Another thing," Carter said, leaning forward until his lips were close to Fernando's ear so he could hear better above the wind. "The plan will be changed a little."

"How so?"

"We might not need Paragem's info after all. I've got the name of the freighter; she's the *Celestial Light*, out of Algiers."

He gave Fernando the freighter's sailing time, and the other man did some calibrations.

"She'll be off Maria Luisa about now."

"Can we hit her before Ponta de Sagres?" Carter asked.

"Easy."

"We also may not have to gamble on the boat. The woman I told you about—Maria 'Coco' Chanette—sailed on the *Celestial Light*."

"So we spot which boat she boards and follow that one?"

"Exactly," Carter nodded. "And I've got just the thing for that as well."

From beneath the leather jacket he wore, Carter produced a small case. He opened it and lifted it before Fernando's eyes. The man looked and shook his head.

"It's a magnetic beeper . . . two of them. They send out a signal we can follow up to five miles."

Fernando nodded grimly. "We may need it. Look!"

Carter followed the other man's arm seaward into the gray splotched darkness. About two miles before them, a haze seemed to lift off the ocean.

"Fog?" Carter asked.

"Patches of it," Fernando replied, "and thick."

"Then we'll definitely need this," Carter said, clasping his fist over the beepers' container. "Are the suits on board?"

"Below," Fernando said, checking his watch. "Also, it's almost time. The radio is on."

Carter nodded and went forward to the hatch. Below, he stripped and climbed into the black wet suit, all the while listening to the radio.

A man's sonorous voice intoned weather and fishing reports in a bored monotone.

When he was finished dressing and transferring Hugo, Wilhelmina, and the beeper box into watertight pockets of the suit, Carter lit up and waited.

He knew the signal would come. Paragem had assured

him that tonight was the night, and the presence of Coco Chanette confirmed it.

But still there was the thrill and exhilaration when the words were said, and Carter knew beyond a doubt that the hunt was on.

". . . and the shrimp are running off Sagres."

ELEVEN

The fog swirled and shifted, moved by the same wind that propelled *O Sombra* through the night. Often they would move out of a fog bank only to have the same blanket of gray overtake and envelop them again.

Twice on the outward leg they had heard the mournful wail of a foghorn. Both times Carter had looked to Fernando, searching the seaman's face questioningly.

Both times the reply had been a shaking head and the words, "Too close to land. A freighter will stay closer to midchannel until she's free of the Cape St. Vincent lighthouse."

Then they had turned east, toward Gibraltar, and that was their heading now.

Carter crouched in the bow, fully rigged now with snorkle, mask, and flippers. With narrowed eyes he searched the grayness and, in a clear space, the foaming sea.

They had been out over two hours, and Carter was getting edgy.

He was just moving down the port side when Fernando raised his hand. "Feel it?"

"Feel what?"

"That vibration . . ."

Carter felt nothing, and nearly lost his footing as Fernando swung the boat hard to port and began tacking.

"There!" he suddenly hissed. "Coming up on our starboard side. Hear it?"

Carter crouched lower to the deck and shut his eyes. With all the power he could muster he concentrated, shutting out all the usual sounds of the sea.

Then he was once more amazed with Fernando's seamanship.

Coming up hard off the starboard bow, Carter heard the steady drone of a big ship's screws.

Again Fernando swung *O Sombra* about until the bigger ship seemed right next to them.

And then it *was* right next to them, not fifty feet off the starboard side, part of its mast and bow looming above the ocean-hugging fog.

She was doing about five knots better than they were and seemed to be slowing. By the time they were amidships, Carter had the night glasses in his hands and Fernando was already inching closer.

Carter could see what the other man was doing. It was unlikely there would be anyone on the fantail who would spot them.

Just when their little boat began to bob and roll in the freighter's wash, Carter raised the glasses and focused.

He saw the stern pass before his eyes, and then he sighted up from the waterline until he found her markings: *Celestial Light* . . . Libya.

"That's her!"

The cry had barely left Carter's mouth when the drone from the freighter's screws changed tone and the water around them began to boil. At the same time, the *Celestial Light*'s foghorn began to wail.

There was a cackle from the stern, and Carter spun in his crouch. Fernando's white teeth gleamed in an ear-to-ear smile.

"What is it?" Carter asked.

"She's reversing, stopping . . . or at least slowing to a crawl. My guess is we're right at the rendezvous point and her horn is calling the chicks into the nest!"

"Goddamn," Carter said in awe, and then a sound beyond Fernando reached his ears.

It was different and more muted than the freighter's churning screws.

"Diesel," Fernando said and rolled the tiller around.

O Sombra caught a gust and leaped ahead. In an instant they were in a fog bank. They were barely shrouded when the sound of another, and yet another, engine reached their ears. As they continued to skim along, the fog suddenly seemed full of engines.

"Lower the mainsail!" Fernando barked, and Carter jumped to the task.

Instantly the boat eased off, bobbing at not more than three knots and slowly tacking.

"All right," Fernando said. "We're about fifty meters off her port side. I'd say about midships."

"How the hell can you tell that?" Carter gasped.

"By her prop wash. Look at the water."

Carter looked.

He couldn't really tell if they were exactly fifty meters off and directly amidships of the *Celestial Light*, but he could see the water alongside *O Sombra* slowly churning and knew that Fernando could read it.

"Go in here," Fernando said. "Take your bearings off the chugging sound of the diesels. Try to stay just in front of them. Keep the sound in your right ear. Got it?"

"Got it," Carter replied, wetting his mask.

"And if I'm wrong about being amidships, you'll know it when you feel the screws start to suck you in. Swim like hell, backward!"

Carter nodded and rolled off the bow into the sea.

He was swimming when he hit the surface, long, clean,

even strokes. Heeding Fernando's advice, he gauged his speed off the sound of the approaching boats.

Once he paid too much attention to an approaching craft from his right and nearly got run down by one from his left. At the last second he dived, felt the small prop churn water barely over his head, and surfaced at last, gasping for air.

Then he was there, right alongside the *Celestial Light* and exactly amidships.

Treading water and nudging his shoulder against the ship's steel side, Carter removed the snorkle and mask from his head and attached them to his belt.

Then he pulled out the small box, removed one of the beepers, and slid it into his mouth under his tongue.

The first fishing boat had already pulled alongside the *Celestial Light*. Carter cursed to himself when he saw a pallet being raised by electric winch from the smaller boat's deck.

The first fishing boat was already loaded.

Was Chanette on it?

Carter could only hope that as gutsy as Coco Chanette was, she wasn't gutsy enough to ride a swaying pallet down the freighter's side along with the crates.

Still treading water, he kept just his forehead and eyes out of the water and watched the operation.

The first boat had barely pulled away from the freighter's side when the pallet was already loaded and being lowered. By the time the second boat was in place, the loaded pallet was only a few feet above its deck.

The operation was smooth, well organized, and well executed.

As each boat came in, a line was also lowered. Carter guessed the man handling that part of the operation was the skipper of the *Celestial Light* himself. A piece of paper would be attached to the line and brought back up to the freighter's deck. The captain would quickly peruse the paper and nod down for the crates to be unloaded.

Carter guessed the papers were some kind of coded vouchers. They had probably been included in the envelopes sent to the fishermen telling them of their unloading points.

On and on it went, and Carter's legs, constantly churning in the water, began to cramp up.

And then the break came.

Boat number six chugged into place. The rope-wound pallet with the usual two crates hovered over her deck. The line came down, the paper was attached, and up it went.

The routine was the same except for a single addition.

After the freighter's captain read the paper and nodded to the boat below, he turned and gestured toward two nearby seamen. Their arms went simultaneously into the air, and over the side came a rope ladder.

The fishing boat's skipper and his hand quickly unloaded the crates, signaled the pallet up, and grabbed the bottom of the ladder.

It was barely in place before a darkly clad figure appeared at the rail. Carter couldn't see the face, but the swell of the hips in a pair of black slacks and the unmistakable twin bulges in the leather jacket told him that the figure was a woman.

She said a few words to the captain, shook his hand, and, unaided, swung over the side.

"Check," Carter whispered to himself. "Let's hope 'Mate' comes later!"

Coco Chanette was halfway down the ladder when Carter dived. Beneath the surface he reset the mask over his eyes and kicked slowly toward the fishing boat's bow. When his groping hands found the barnacled timbers, he surfaced again.

Perfect.

He was bobbing just under the far side of the bow. Even if someone on the freighter were looking, they wouldn't be able to see him.

The only problem was finding metal on the boat to which to attach the beeper's magnet.

Slowly he moved along the side. The boat was wood. All wood. There were three sets of oar locks, but Carter couldn't reach them.

There was only one sure place.

Carter dived. He found the mainstem, kept his shoulder against it for guidance, and followed it aft.

The vibration from the slowly turning screw sent shivers of caution up his spine, and he inched his hands along the boat's bottom.

Can't go too far, he thought grimly, *or it's fingers for the cause!*

He felt the suck from the screw, paused, and moved his hands upward.

His fingers touched and then curled around the rudder housing.

It was metal.

Holding on with his left hand, Carter brought his right to his mouth. Carefully he slipped his thumb and forefinger beneath his tongue and got a good hold on the beeper before extracting it.

Just as carefully, he found his left hand with the fingers of his right and moved a few inches aft on the housing.

He couldn't hear the click of the magnet grabbing, but he could feel the pull and knew it was secure.

And just in time.

The thudding vibration of the diesel increased and the water around him began to churn.

The boat was loaded and pulling out.

The prop couldn't have been more than a six-incher, but it was generating one hell of a lot of suction.

Carter dipped his head and relaxed. He could feel himself rising to the surface. He kept his palms flat against the side of the boat and his legs straight out behind him, away from the prop.

When he felt his butt break the surface, he pushed off and paddled backward with all his might. At the same time, he raised his head for one quick look and a much-needed gulp of air.

One man was at the tiller, and a second was rigging sail. The boat was already clipping along, and there was no sign of Chanette.

Carter guessed she was already below.

He dived again, did a cartwheel beneath the surface, and started swimming. Again he took his bearings off the engines of the boats still being loaded. When he was sure he couldn't be spotted from the freighter, he came to the surface and changed his stroke to a crawl.

When he figured about fifty yards, he stopped and waited.

If the beepers were working—one in his wet suit and one on Chanette's boat—Fernando should find him in no time.

The seconds became minutes, and Carter's legs started to feel like logs. He let himself go limp so he would float and kept one ear out of the water, listening for the gentle slap of Fernando's boat's bow against the waves.

And then he heard it, about twenty feet to his right.

The beeper worked fine.

Three strokes and *O Sombra*'s bow loomed directly over him.

The fog grew thicker as they sailed out parallel to the coastline.

But it mattered little.

The beeper signal was coming in loud and clear, and Fernando's uncanny instincts did the rest.

Like the boat they followed, *O Sombra* now ran under full sail and diesel power.

"Falésia," Fernando suddenly growled.

"What?"

"Falésia," he repeated. "It is a beach area near Vilamoura. There are many small coves and inlets near there, but only two have good access up the cliffs."

"You think that's where they're going?" Carter asked.

"That is my guess, but we'll soon know for sure."

On the bow, Carter turned his head toward the coastline. Anxiously he peered through the mist. The sound of the signal was so clear now he thought they surely must be right on top of the other boat.

Fernando wheeled the boat around until her bow was headed directly for the cliffs. At the same time, he cut the diesel and began a slow tack.

"I hear them," Carter hissed.

The sound of the other boat's engine was faint but distinct somewhere about a hundred yards off the port bow.

Carter glanced back.

Fernando was intent. His hand handled the tiller with confidence. His head was cocked to the side, his ear reading the nuances of sound that came to them over the water.

Suddenly the sound from the other diesel stopped.

"They're in," Fernando announced, and again *O Sombra*'s bow came around.

"You know the cove? Which one, I mean?" Carter asked.

"*Sim*. We will land at Falésia and ride the coast road back."

"Can we make it in time?"

"With time to spare, *mon ami*," came the reply.

Minutes later the boat's bow kissed the sand and both men were over the side, pulling and tugging. With the help of the ocean, ten feet of the boat's hull was beached in no time.

While Fernando tied up his craft, Carter unlashed the two BMWs. Together they set the plank, and then the machines were roaring with life.

Carter followed Fernando off, hit the sand, and they were hill climbing up a steep path all the way to the top of the cliff.

"Follow me!" Fernando called over his shoulder, and Carter fell directly in behind him.

The two motorcycles' headbeams cut the night like knives as they roared inland over what looked like a goat path. When Fernando veered left, Carter followed suit.

In no time they had covered six miles through olive and pecan groves, tilled fields, and two villages of a few huts and shops.

Fernando signaled, and Carter throttled down.

"Lights!" he said.

Both beams went off, and minutes later the machines came to a halt side by side.

"We'll go the rest of the way on foot," Fernando said, already moving over the rocks and huge boulders like a goat.

Carter was proud of himself when he only stumbled ten times following the giant over the rugged terrain.

At last they reached a rocky outcropping where Carter could hear the sound of the sea directly below them. The area around where they stood, and all along the cliff before them, was clear. The sea, the beach, and the rocks below were still obscured by fog.

"There!" Fernando said, pointing.

Carter saw them: three men working a hand winch at the edge of the cliff. A cranelike arm extended about ten feet from the rim, and lines from it disappeared down into the fog.

"There is a tiny restaurant on the beach below," Fernando explained. "During working hours, the winch is used to lower supplies so they don't have to be manhandled down the path."

For several moments they watched the men at work hauling and tugging on the lines.

And then a wooden pallet, secured by ropes at its four

corners, appeared above the cliff. On the pallet were the two crates Carter had seen unloaded earlier.

Just as the arm was swinging in, Coco Chanette appeared on the path leading up from the beach. She seemed to materialize out of the fog like a black specter with a stark white face.

She now carried a briefcase in her hand.

Carter guessed that it had been loaded on the fishing boat while he was underwater attaching the beeper.

Chanette reached the three men. They talked in low tones for a few seconds, and then the stillness of the night was broken by the sounds of engines.

From the inland road to their right, a small Renault sedan and a truck emerged from an olive grove.

"Come," Fernando whispered, "we will meet them where this road comes out on the highway."

"Are you sure it's the only way out?" Carter asked.

"*Mon ami*, the Algarve is my home. I know every goat path and all the ones that have been widened into roads. Hurry!"

They raced back to the BMWs and quickly kicked them into life.

Again, Fernando was unerring.

To Carter they seemed to be heading directly toward the cliff and the sea, but in no time they came out on the main highway.

Fernando roared on across it into yet another grove of trees, and immediately they started climbing. Finally Fernando halted and killed his machine.

"Perfect," Carter said.

They were in a grove of pecan trees on a ridge looking right down at the highway and the dirt road leading to the beach.

"They come!"

Carter saw the lights at nearly the same time he heard the engines. He took the binoculars from their case and trained them on the moving vehicles.

The truckdriver was alone.

The three men who had hoisted the crates were in the Renault with Chanette.

When they reached the main highway, the truck turned right, toward Faro.

The Renault went left.

"The woman is yours, Fernando. I'll take the truck!"

"*Sim,*" the big man replied, the machine between his legs already sputtering to life.

TWELVE

Within a very few miles, Carter could tell that the driver of the truck was only a hireling, a man who probably suspected that the load he had picked up from the beach at night was probably illegal. But he obviously could care less.

He drove steadily, paying no attention behind him and attempting no evasive maneuvers.

As they neared the city limits of Faro, Carter turned on the BMW's headlight.

Traffic was almost nil, so Carter had little trouble trailing the truck at a distance.

On through Faro they went, and again they were on the main highway. Carter went over the map of the Algarve he had implanted in his brain. About eighteen miles beyond Faro was the town of Tavira. That was it until the Spanish frontier.

Carter leaned forward, relaxing over the BMW's handlebars.

Eighteen miles, twenty minutes.

Tavira was it.

At the city square, the truck turned right. Carter followed, still at a distance, until the truck slowed and then stopped at a large iron gate.

Carter kicked the stand down, leaned the bike into it, and ran the rest of the way.

The gate was open, and the truck was already backed up to a loading dock.

Above the gate was a rusty tin sign: MONTEGA AND SONS LTD, SEAFOOD EXPORTERS.

Carter darted through the gate and hit the wall of loading docks. The truck was three docks away. Above it was a single bulb, giving no more light than was needed for the unloading process.

Staying low, Carter moved one dock closer and then settled into the darkness under the ramp to wait.

Five minutes later, the corrugated door rolled up and three men stepped out. It was the driver and two dock workers. They were all carrying coffee cups and speaking in Portuguese.

Carter caught just enough to tell that the gist of the conversation was that it was a bitch that Paragem always sent his shipments at such an ungodly hour.

So, Carter thought, José Paragem had been holding back on him. Evidently the fat man did have more to do with the operation than he had been willing to tell Carter that afternoon.

This was partially confirmed when the men started unloading.

Carter stopped counting at thirty-five crates, all identically marked, and started looking for a way into the building.

He found it on the roof, an unlocked door that led to a stairway, which in turn came out on a catwalk above the floor of a huge warehouse.

The unlocked door figured. The inside of the warehouse reeked of fish. Who would want to steal fish?

Carter watched the last crate come off the truck. While one of the dockworkers wheeled it inside, the second one counted the crates with the driver. When this was done, both men signed a paper attached to a clipboard.

The driver accepted his receipt and was gone out the door, which quickly closed behind him.

Seconds later Carter heard the truck start up and drive away.

The two dockworkers split. One left using a door into the night, and the other mounted some stairs at the opposite end of the building from where Carter crouched.

At the top he hung the clipboard on a wall alongside several others. At a wall panel, he killed the big floods that had been illuminating the warehouse, leaving only small nightlights.

Then he passed through a door into what looked like an office.

Carter waited ten minutes and then moved around the catwalk. Light from a low-wattage bulb gleamed through the frosted pane of the door.

Cautiously, Carter raised himself until he could peer into the room. Even though the glass was frosted, he could still make out images. There were two desks with chairs, a few file cabinets, and a cot.

Evidently the man wasn't too afraid of burglary.

Heavy snoring was already emanating through the door.

Carter searched until he found the right clipboard. When he did, he removed all the papers from it and crept silently down the stairs. When he reached the warehouse's main floor, he moved back under the catwalk and rescued a penlight from one of the wet suit's pockets.

There were forty-one crates in all, on consignment from Paragem's firm in Portimão and two other brokers along the Algarve.

The entire shipment was due to be sent out the following morning by ship to Marseille. From there the shipment was to be flown by commercial freight liner. Its end lease read: U.S. Army, NATO Command, Brussels, Belgium.

It was neat. Very neat. Paragem shipped through Montega and Sons, and somebody at the other end spotted the right crates and pulled them before the seafood was dispersed.

Carter was willing to bet Montega and Sons were legit and clean. They probably shipped for every seafood broker in the Algarve.

But if that was the case, where did *the man* fit in?

Coco Chanette grew the stuff, refined and cut it, and shipped it out of Algiers.

Paragem picked it up and shipped it through Montega and Sons Ltd.

What did *the man* do, if anything, beyond pulling Paragem's strings?

Carter pocketed the papers and moved to the crates. One by one he went over them with the penlight. Twenty-three of the crates had been brokered through Paragem's company.

Carter was going over the twelfth crate when he spotted the difference in the markings.

It was on the end destination marking: NATO COMMAND.

On two of the crates, command was spelled COMAND.

It was a logical error that a clerk in another country, speaking and writing little or no English, would make.

Carter searched until he found a loading hook and, as quietly as possible, pried open one of the designated crates. The stench hit him immediately, but there was nothing for it. Pausing every minute or so to move away and gulp in air, he unloaded the crate fish by fish, chunk of dry ice by chunk of dry ice.

No package. No oilskin bag. No nothing.

Slowly Carter played the narrow beam over the floor where he had laid out the fish and the ice.

Still nothing.

He was just reaching for the loading hook to pry open the second crate, when something hit his eye.

Certain chunks of the dry ice seemed to have a whiter hue emanating from their centers than did others.

Carter chose two of them and slid them across the floor to the exit. Quickly he picked the door lock and, gingerly bouncing the two chunks, went out onto the loading dock. He shut the door behind him to further muffle the sound, and fished out Wilhelmina.

Using the butt of the Luger, he pounded both chunks apart.

Ingenious.

There, frozen into the center of the dry ice, was a fine, white powder.

One taste told Carter it was heroin.

A whole new wrinkle on smuggling, he thought. If something went wrong or delayed the shipment, the ice would eventually melt. The heroin would filter down, becoming one with a load of smelly fish that would only too soon be disposed of.

No telltale bags or oilskin covers for these smugglers. Either the heroin got there or it disappeared.

Back inside, Carter scrounged around the warehouse until he found a small canvas bag. He joined the broken chunks with two fresh ones, and spent the next fifteen minutes reloading and securing the crate.

Then he very carefully relocked the door and left the way he had entered, by the roof.

He wanted to give them no warning that he had gained as much knowledge as he had.

Carter sailed past the gas station, barely glancing at the sedan parked beside it beneath the trees.

The boys were back at their post.

That meant Leonita was in.

He left the main highway at Lagoa and took the smaller road down to Carvoeiro. Just past the Long Bar, he spotted the black Mercedes back in its spot behind the café.

The men in it barely glanced up as Carter sped by on the BMW and climbed the hill to the villa.

But then, why should they? They had seen Fernando ride up this same hill on a BMW several times in the last two days. And in the darkness they wouldn't even notice the wet suit Carter was wearing.

Carter drove clear around the house and stashed the BMW in the shed.

He was halfway across the patio when Lars appeared from some shrubbery at the side of the house. The Galil assault rifle in his hands looked big, black, and ugly.

"Just making sure no strangers were out riding black BMWs tonight," he said with a chuckle, clicking on the rifle's safety. "How did it go?"

"A picnic," Carter replied, holding up the canvas bag. "I even got samples. You?"

"They never suspected, I'm sure of it. Although they must think you are crazy to drive halfway to Lisbon, have a glass of wine, and drive back."

They both entered the rear glass doors of the villa laughing.

Leonita was sound asleep on the living room sofa. Carter would wake her, but one call had to be made first.

It took a full five minutes for the international operator in Lisbon to reach the States. From there it was only seconds to Dupont Circle and Ginger Bateman.

"Put this on a scrambler," Carter said.

"Right."

Garbled growls, static, and then a high-pitched whine hit Carter's ears, and then Ginger's voice came through. "You're on. Go!"

"Is the man in?"

"No, but I think I've got what you want."

"Craylon?"

"Right. He's back in Brussels, and he'll be in his office in the morning."

"Good. Reconfirm that, and put a high priority on making sure the brigadier's ass is indeed in his office in the morning."

"You're flying in?"

"Like a bird," Carter replied. "Have you got the name of a security honcho at NATO Brussels who has brains and clout?"

"One minute." She was back in ten seconds. "Colonel John S. Meyers. He's good."

"He's going to have to be," Carter said. "Give my love to Washington."

"Tally-ho!" she replied, and the line went dead.

Carter turned and moved to the sofa. Leonita's eyes blinked wide when Carter brushed his lips across her forehead.

"I'm home from the office, dear," he said. "Did you have a nice day?"

"Splendid. I had a leisurely drive to Faro, an even more leisurely dinner, picked up two nasty-looking guns in a suitcase from Camilla, and got back for the evening news."

"Were you chaperoned all the way?"

"I certainly was. I imagine they are starving. I did not give them a lunch break. Want to go to bed?"

"Can't," Carter replied. "I think I have a bit of flying to do."

Her lips formed a pout as she rolled her face back into the sofa.

Carter turned to Lars. "Has Fernando checked in yet?"

"About a half hour ago."

Carter fixed himself a scotch and settled in with the phone.

Fernando answered on the first ring.

"Tell me you didn't lose her, my friend."

"No way." The big man laughed. "I think I could have

ridden the BMW right up their tailpipe and they wouldn't have paid any attention. No, *mon ami*, as far as they were concerned, I was out fishing and you were joyriding around Portugal!''

''I had the same with the truck,'' Carter replied, and he filled the big fisherman in on what he had discovered.

''*Merde*, Nick, you had a much more interesting evening than I.''

''How so?''

''There is a small winery in the hills above Silves. Actually it is an old Moorish castle that was converted many years ago.''

''That's where they went?''

''And stayed,'' Fernando replied.

''Who owns the winery?''

''It was a co-op until a few years ago. They met with bad times, and the place went to seed. I had heard that a foreign company had bought the castle and land about two years ago, but I didn't know that the winery was again in operation.''

''And it is?'' Carter asked, concentrating, trying to put the pieces of the puzzle together in his mind.

''Definitely. There is smoke pouring from the chimneys, so the cookers are working, and the aroma of fermentation hangs like jasmine in the air around the place.''

''Jesus,'' Carter chuckled, ''you're a poet.''

''Of course! I'm Portuguese . . . my soul is filled with sadness!'' To emphasize it, Fernando roared with laughter.

''Can you find out who is operating the winery now?''

''*Sim*, first thing in the morning. I have a crooked friend who is a lawyer in the Silves land use department.''

''Good. Also, in the morning you'd better bring Camilla up here. Let's put the whole gang under one roof until D-day.''

''I will do it. Also, I have many donkey-driver friends . . .''

"Yes . . .?"

"Even now they watch the winery with their beady little eyes to see if the woman leaves. You will be at the villa in the morning?"

"No, I'm flying."

"When?"

"Tonight," Carter sighed, "as soon as I can get a bird."

"Fly fast and safe, and return to us soon. I'm beginning to enjoy the excitement you put into this old smuggler's life!"

"And the money."

"*Sim*, very much the money! *Adeus!*"

"*Adeus*, my friend."

Carter broke the connection and dialed the Lisbon AXE number.

A machine answered, giving Carter MacHugh's private number.

"Yeah?"

"Carter here."

"Jesus, it's four o'clock in the morning!" MacHugh's voice was like a fingernail going across slate.

"It's four-thirty," Carter growled. "How'd our delivery go?"

"Like clockwork. I should have the results by noon tomorrow."

"Good. I've got another piece to run through the same tests. I'll leave it at the air base."

"What air base?"

"The NATO air base here in Portugal where you have that plane at my disposal. You do have it, don't you, Mac?"

"How soon do you need it?"

"About seven o'clock."

"Jesus, don't you ever sleep?"

"About the same amount of time you stay sober."

"I'll call flight ops."

"Good. I'll call you tomorrow from Brussels."

"Brother, some pilot is going to shit."

Carter hung up and headed for the stairs. He showered away the odor of fish and sea, and climbed into a fresh, lightweight suit.

Back downstairs, he met Lars who dangled the keys to one of the Fiestas on a finger.

"Take good care of her, okay?"

"You know I will," Lars said, patting the Galil.

"I know this isn't your line of work, Lars. Thanks."

The man shrugged. "What you're paying me is more than ten runs to Morocco. Believe me, American, I'm not bitching."

"*Adeus.*"

Two minutes later Carter came off the hill in the Fiesta. He was across the square and turning onto the Lagoa road when the lights of the Mercedes came on behind him.

"My, oh my, fellows," Carter said aloud, "but you're in for another long drive and wait!"

THIRTEEN

His name was Major Marc Gaston. He was a good pilot, and he didn't ask any questions.

Rightly so, he figured that if a civilian tough-type like Nick Carter had the clout to commandeer an Air Force jet, and his services to fly it to Brussels, he must be somebody.

No more than ten words passed between them the entire trip.

Carter had barely hit the tarmac when he was barking orders to a young captain who met the plane.

"I want this plane refueled and ready to go in two hours, preferably one. And get me a staff command car and driver."

"That might be a little difficult."

"Captain, I didn't ask you how. I said, do it."

The captain looked to Gaston for support. It was in his eyes: *Who does this guy think he is?*

Gaston shrugged.

Carter jumped back in.

"I've got a Security One, Pentagon clearance," he said. "And I haven't got all day."

Five minutes later Nick Carter was sitting in a staff car beside a white-faced sergeant speeding across Brussels.

The NATO headquarters building was on the edge of the city, away from the military compound itself.

Carter stepped from the car and leaned back through the window. "Get some coffee if you want, Sergeant, but don't stray far or for very long from this vehicle."

"Yes, sir."

NATO Special Services took up the sixth and seventh floors of the building. Brigadier General Jeremy S. Craylon's office was on the seventh.

Carter stepped from the elevator and zeroed in on it.

Craylon's secretary was a little blond lieutenant who looked bored, and sounded it when Carter announced himself.

"You'll have to take a seat, sir. The general is on a long-distance call."

"What's your name, Lieutenant?'

"Finch, sir."

"Well, Finch, you tell the general his call is canceled."

"I . . . I can't do that, sir."

"I can," Carter barked, heading for the inner office door. "Get Colonel Meyers of NATO Security on the phone and tell him to get his ass over here. And hold all the rest of General Craylon's calls."

"You can't go in . . ."

But Carter was already inside the office and slamming the door behind him.

Brigadier General Jeremy S. Craylon sat behind a desk a little less than two miles wide and a mile deep, with a phone screwed into his ear.

Craylon was about fifty, give or take a year, and egg-shaped, with the narrow part at the shoulders. He had an earnest, fleshy face, and his wiry, curling hair was receding clear to the crown. His jacket was off, and his khaki uniform shirt was soaked at the armpits.

And they're going to be a lot damper, Carter thought, *by the time I'm through with him.*

Craylon was wide-eyed and on his feet by the time Carter hit the desk.

"Who the hell . . .?"

"Nick Carter. How important is that call?"

"It's my wife."

"Tell her good-bye."

"Like hell I will!" Craylon sputtered.

Carter wrenched the phone from his hand and brought it to his own lips. "Mrs. Craylon . . .?"

"Yes," came the surprised reply.

"Good-bye."

Carter dropped the phone back to its cradle and studied Craylon while he lit a cigarette.

"I don't know who the hell you think you are, mister . . ."

"I told you. Nick Carter."

". . . and I don't allow smoking in this office!"

He pointed to a sign on his desk: THANK YOU FOR NOT SMOKING.

Carter stepped on the cigarette, then fumbled with the false heel of his shoe. Craylon sputtered some more and again reached for the phone, presumably to call the marines. When Carter had the heel pushed aside, he withdrew a plastic ID card and dropped it on the desk in front of the general.

The card was the kind of identification Carter rarely used. It mentioned nothing of AXE, but it did sport his picture and a carte blanche clearance from a very high authority, an authority that drained the color from the general's face and dropped his lower lip to his navel.

He dropped the phone and eased his wide bottom half back into his chair.

Carter leaned across the desk and poked a button on the intercom. "Finch?"

"Yes, sir," came the frightened WAC's voice.

"When Meyers gets here, send him right in."

"Yes, sir."

Carter sat down himself and Craylon found his voice. It was shaky, but it made words.

"What do you want?"

"What do you know about Montega and Sons, Limited, out of Tavira, Portugal?"

"Nothing. I've never heard of them."

"That's odd," Carter said, curling his lips into a grin that was more like a leer. "You've been importing heroin from them once a month for a long time now."

Up Craylon came again. "Jesus . . ."

"Sit down, Brigadier General, you'll have a coronary. Montega and Sons buy fish from several brokers in the Algarve. One of those brokers is—or was—a man named José Paragem. Paragem was a cog in an international dope ring geared to feed the arms of NATO troops."

"Preposterous . . ."

"Like hell it is. The heroin was concealed in dry ice and shipped to you in crates of fish. Someone at this end, probably in your dispersal section, caught it, and through your distribution to NCO and officers' clubs, moved it all around Europe."

Craylon might have gotten fat in his job, but he didn't get to be a general without some brains. His jaw locked, and a military sternness slipped like a mask over his face.

"You're sure of this?"

"Positive. And I've got the proof."

Craylon's hand whipped across the desk to the intercom. "Lieutenant . . ."

"Yes, sir?"

"Bring me the file on one of our seafood suppliers . . ." He paused, rolling his eyes up to Nick.

"Montega and Sons."

"Montega and Sons, in Portugal," Craylon echoed.

"Right away, sir. And, sir . . .?"

"Yes?"

Finch lowered her voice conspiratorially. "I've called Security, sir. They're here in the outer—"

"Tell them to go back to their office, and bring me that goddamned file."

Carter could hear blunt heels going like hell on the tile of the outside office floor. Then Lieutenant Finch burst through the door.

Carter lifted the file from her hand in passing before she reached the desk and Craylon.

It took about five minutes to peruse the file. Any and all Armed Forces suppliers—domestic or foreign—are checked thoroughly before they can do business with the U.S. government.

Montego and Sons Ltd. was no exception.

Just as Carter thought, they were clean. It was a family firm that went back over sixty years. There wasn't a hint in any part of their past that would link them to the deal.

"Damn," Carter muttered, tossing the folder on the desk.

"Something?" Craylon asked.

"Nothing, and that bodes good for you, General. It's ten-to-one if Montego didn't know they were shipping the stuff, you didn't know you were receiving it."

The sigh of relief was very audible from the opposite side of the desk.

Carter was just standing to pace and think when another officer entered the room. Carter took one look and trusted him immediately.

He was lanky but moved with perfect muscular control, placing his feet on the carpet like a cat, with hardly any effort. His blue eyes and wavy blond hair were movie star, but his mouth and chin were career army.

And the ribbons said experience.

"Colonel Meyers?" Carter said, extending his hand.

"Yes. John Meyers."

He had a firm grip and didn't waste time shaking; one

pump and he was through. He was also calm, waiting for Carter to make the move.

That was good.

"My name's Nick Carter."

He flashed the card. Meyers swallowed it with his eyes and nodded.

"It's your show."

"Good," Carter said and then began to pace. In short, staccato sentences, he retold the tale to Meyers just about the way he had related it to Craylon. But this time he added the spice of Coco Chanette and the "mystery man" element.

When he was finished, Meyers asked no perfunctory questions. He had digested it all, and already had made decisions and come to conclusions.

"I take it that since you let the latest shipment go through, you want me to intercept it at this end?"

"Right," Carter replied. "I'm sure General Craylon will give you all the cooperation you need." He cocked an eyebrow in the general's direction.

"Definitely," came the quick reply.

"If you can wrap up this end," Carter continued, "I'll try to kill the operation from the other end. Plant people around those crates and you should snag 'em like bees when they head for the honey."

"I'll get on it right away," Meyers said and stood to leave.

"One more thing, Colonel . . ."

"Yes?"

"This is probably the last shipment through their regular channel, but I've got reason to believe there might be one more. I'm going to try to nip it, but I'll keep you alerted in case I miss."

"Good enough."

The colonel saluted the general, shook Carter's hand, and left.

"May I use your phone, General?" Carter asked, fishing his wallet from his pocket.

"Of course."

Craylon was out of his chair like a shot. Carter could have dialed from the other side of the desk, but he didn't argue and moved into the man's chair.

As the phone in the Lisbon AXE office rang, Carter did an idle scan of the desk. His eye fell across the usual family picture—Craylon, the wife, and three good-looking kids, two boys and a girl.

"Nice-looking family."

"Thank you," Craylon replied nervously. "Both boys are headed for the Point."

MacHugh picked up on the other end, taking Carter's attention back to the phone.

"Carter. What's the word from Lisbon?"

"Dynamite, but weird."

"How so?"

"It was heroin, all right, and top-grade stuff. Also, it wasn't cut that much."

"You sound like there's more."

"There is, Nick. Do you think this is part of the stuff that's getting to NATO bases around Europe?"

"Some of it is," Carter replied, sensing the sudden solemnity that had crept into the other man's voice. "I'm not sure where those two particular kilos were headed. My source claims they're part of a special shipment."

"They're special, all right. Both kilos have been laced through with a virus."

Carter's hand holding the phone tingled. "What kind of a virus?"

"A form of hepatitis, but ten times stronger than normal. The boys in Madrid couldn't classify it, but they did some animal tests and the stuff is a real killer. The rats had degenerative brain and liver damage far faster and deadlier than could be caused by any known strain. Also, it's almost three times more infectious than any known hepatitis virus.''

''Good God,'' Carter whispered. ''If twenty kilos of that stuff got through . . .''

''Right,'' MacHugh said. ''A dogface wouldn't even have to be a user to buy a ticket to the farm.''

''You're a good man, Mac. Head for the Algarve. I'll see you there.''

''Right.''

Carter sat for several minutes with his face in his hands.

Now it was all too clear why an agriculturist and biologist like Maria ''Coco'' Chanette—who was also trained KGB—was in the game.

The actual heroin ring was only a setup for the big shipment.

And the big shipment was about to take place.

Whoever *the man* was, he was probably responsible for setting up the distribution at the NATO end. That meant he had military ties, and the kind that would get him close to Craylon's office.

But Craylon was clean. Carter was sure of it.

Just as he was about to stand, Carter's eyes strayed across the desk to another photo. It had been taken in Washington, near the base of Lincoln's statue. It was of two men, both in uniform. One was a slightly younger and thinner Jeremy Craylon. The other was a taller, more wiry man with heavy shoulders and much sharper features.

He was obviously a good deal younger than Craylon, but his hair was a premature gray, an arresting silver-gray that seemed to glow in the sunlight.

On closer inspection of the photo, Carter could see captain's bars on the man's shoulders.

''Who's this, General?''

''My brother, Myles. He was my adjutant during my last tour in Washington.''

There was something in the general's tone that tickled Carter's curiosity.

"You don't sound like he was a very good adjutant."

"He wasn't," the general said and sighed. "Oh, not that he wasn't a good soldier . . . he was. As a fighting man I think he was far more a soldier than I ever was. But Myles couldn't take orders, and he was bored with regular army life. I rather expected it. He was rather wild—a Peck's bad boy—at an early age, and I guess he just never grew up."

"Is he stationed with you? . . . here in Brussels?"

"No. He resigned his commission right after that picture was taken. I guess the army just wasn't exciting enough for him, and he had a fondness for a lifestyle that army pay could never allow. He became a mercenary, first in South America and then in central Africa."

The hair on the back of Carter's neck rose, and his hand, holding the photo, began to shake.

The general rattled on about his brother Myles Craylon, but Carter heard very little of it.

Mercenary in central Africa. . . .

Military ties. . . .

A desire for wealth. . . .

"General . . ." Carter rasped, cutting the other man off in mid-sentence.

"Yes?"

"Where is Myles now?"

"Well, he's finally got himself straightened out, and I hope has settled down. He's gone into business."

"What kind of business?"

"He bought a winery in southern Portugal. I hope you won't think it's nepotism, but I've agreed to buy a large shipment of his first year's product . . ."

Carter didn't hear the rest. He was already out the door and heading for the elevator.

Going through his mind was Ines's description to Jorge

Silva of one of Paragem's two constant visitors at the villa.

One of them was a tall, good-looking, silver-haired man.

But Ines never heard the man speak, so she couldn't know that he was American.

FOURTEEN

There were several lights on in the winery's top stories. From a nearby hillside, Carter and Fernando could see movement behind two of the windows.

"What do your donkey drivers say?" Carter asked.

"The man you describe is there, inside with the woman. There are only three others, all armed."

Carter nodded, idly running his hand along the Galil.

"You've sent your friends away?"

"*Sim,*" Fernando replied. "They have been well paid, as you said, and will remember nothing of what they have seen here at the winery."

"Good. Give me the layout."

"The cellar is a storage area. The center courtyard and the first floor is the winery itself. The second floor holds offices and living quarters."

"Okay, I'm going in."

"I would like to accompany you, *mon ami.*"

Carter smiled. "I know you would, but you've done enough. Just cover my ass from up here if any of the others come back."

"You are going to arrest them?"

It was a silly question and both men knew it. Fernando had already weighed this hard-eyed American who barked orders and moved through the night like a cat.

Policemen arrest people.

Fernando knew that Nick Carter was no policeman.

Carter answered him anyway.

"If they were arrested, Fernando, there would be a trial, a judge, a jury. And if they were convicted, they might go to prison."

Fernando nodded. "But eventually they would be released."

"Exactly. I am their judge and jury, Fernando. That's why I go in and you stay out."

Silently Carter slipped into the darkness and made his way down the hill.

The castle had been built into the side of a hill. It was a straight drop down one side, with the rear and the other side thickly bordered by trees. There was one road that led up to the gate. The gate itself opened into the center courtyard.

There was only one bad thing about the night: it was clear, with a bright moon.

But once inside, Carter figured that would help rather than hinder him.

And on the outside, he was one with the trees and invisible as he moved parallel to the road in the shadows.

He had already spotted one man on the parapets with a rifle. A second was near the main gate, lounging and smoking.

Carter guessed—and hoped—that the third was somewhere in the bowels of the building asleep, waiting for his turn at the watch.

Carter stopped thirty yards shy of the gate, short-strapped the Galil's sling, and slid it over his shoulder and back. Then he eased down an embankment into a creek that ran parallel to the road.

Silently he waded through the knee-high water. The front wall was directly above him. The mud was like ooze on the embankment here, making for lousy footing. But with the help of vines and a few scrub pines, he made the top and moved along the wall.

The sentry was perched on a stool just inside the gate. Carter couldn't believe his luck. The man's rifle was five feet from him, leaning against the wall.

Carter activated the spring in Hugo's sheath and felt the stiletto's narrow hilt slip into his palm. He had already fit a silencer to Wilhelmina for close, quiet work, but he wanted this one alive long enough to give Carter the information he needed.

Slowly he backpedaled and moved slightly to his left. He had a perfect line now on the huge, open oak door, the man, and his rifle. Carter raised Hugo above his head, took a deep breath, and threw.

The aim was perfect.

Hugo's point made a thudding sound in the wood, shoulder-high, halfway between the sentry and his rifle.

The man was off the stool in an instant, going for the rifle. Carter charged into the center of the road just under the arch of the wall.

The man paused, his concentration drawn by Carter from the rifle. It was for only a second, but that was long enough for Carter to cover the ten yards between them.

Just as the sentry reached his rifle, Carter reached him. Without halting his momentum, Carter brought his elbow around in an arc. It connected solidly with the side of the man's head, slamming him against the door.

Before he rolled away, Carter reached up and behind him, filling his hand with Hugo. In a heartbeat he had grabbed a handful of the other's hair with his left hand, yanking back and bringing Hugo's point against his Adam's apple.

"*Parlez-vous français?*" Carter hissed.

"*Oui,*" the man replied, his eyes a yard wide and the pupils huge as they stared at Hugo's steel catching the moonlight.

"The silver-haired man and the woman . . . where?"

"Second floor, right wing," he gasped as Carter parted the skin of his throat just a hair.

"How many rooms?"

"Two in front . . . and a bath, I think. I've only been up there once."

"I saw another sentry in the tower parapet. Where's your third compadre?"

"Sleeping, there in the cooker room behind that door."

His arm came up slowly, the finger pointing, and Carter made it.

"When is the shipment moving out?"

"I don't know . . . but we don't work after tomorrow."

"That's what I needed to know," Carter growled, pulling Hugo away from the man's throat and sliding the point down across his chest to the bottom of his rib cage.

Relief flooded the man's face as Carter counted five ribs back up and buried two inches of the stiletto in his heart.

Carefully Carter propped him back on the stool and made his way to the cooker room door.

Once there, Carter slid Hugo back into the sheath and pulled Wilhelmina from under his arm.

He slid the door open a crack, just enough to see inside. It was a small room with a large arch in its far wall that led to what had once been the castle's great room. There, Carter could see the huge vats and piping of the winery itself.

The second sentry lay sprawled, fully dressed, across a cot. One arm was thrown over his eyes to shield them from the light of a candle on a nearby, rough-hewn table. A machine pistol lay on the floor by the cot within easy reach.

As Carter stepped into the room, his foot brushed some loose gravel on the stone floor.

"Maurice . . .?"

"*Oui,*" Carter growled, leveling the long silencer over his left forearm.

Obviously the guy knew Maurice's voice. He came off the cot like a shot, fumbling for the weapon.

Carter squeezed off two shots that made a *phffft* sound as Wilhelmina bucked in his hand.

He would have needed only one. It caught the man dead center in the forehead. The second made a mess out of the side of his neck.

Carter snuffed the candle, closed the door, and made for the other side of the courtyard.

He constantly eyed the far tower as he darted through the array of barrels, vats, wagons, and carts that littered the old cobblestones.

Pausing only long enough to flatten all the tires on a Mercedes sedan, Carter reached the wide stone stairs that led up to the top of the wall.

Once on the top, he paused . . . listening. Thirty seconds, a minute went by, and then two.

Carter was about to take a chance and move on around the tower walkway for contact, when he heard the click of a cigarette lighter above him.

He looked up. The man had left the lower walkway and gone up into the tower itself. He now stood, outlined against the moon, smoking and gazing out over the trees.

It would have been the easiest shot in the world, like picking a squirrel out of a tree with a scope.

But Carter preferred to wait.

Eventually it paid off. The cigarette went over the side like a firefly, spiriting down out of sight over the wall.

And then Carter heard the steady thud of booted feet on the stone steps.

He holstered Wilhelmina and moved into the shadows across from the bottom of the steps. The Galil slipped easily off his shoulder, and Carter crouched, holding it across his chest.

The steps grew louder, and then the man was at the bottom.

It was Nikko.

Carter stepped forward, thrusting the Galil's barrel under Nikko's bandaged chin and into his throat.

"What the—" the man gasped, his hands coming up instinctively to shove the rifle aside.

"Don't do it, Nikko," Carter hissed, and he stepped into the moonlight.

"Carter! How . . .?"

". . . did I get here without your flunkies at the villa spotting me leaving?"

"Yeah," he rasped, his eyes rolling from one side to the other looking for an avenue of escape.

"They're dead, Nikko, and all nicely parked in Fernando's boat. Maurice and your man in the cooker room joined 'em in hell about five minutes ago."

Even in the moonlight Carter could see the color drain from Nikko's face.

"You're an American, Nikko. How did you get involved in this?"

"I'm a Sicilian now," he replied in a shaky voice. "I was deported three years ago."

"Along with Carlo?"

"Yeah."

"And the others?"

"Algerian. They work for the broad."

"But you work for Craylon."

Nikko's eyes grew wide, telling a lot of tales. Craylon's identity was the big deal, the big secret. If Carter knew who Craylon was, the party was over.

"Yeah. I met him a long time ago. Ran some guns to him in Africa."

"Do you know who the woman is?"

"Her name's Chanette. She works with Craylon."

Carter smiled. "You think that's all she does?"

"What else? She grows and ships; we distribute."

Carter believed him. But it made no difference. Even if Nikko knew the whole story, he would feel little patriotism for the country that had booted him out.

"Who killed your buddy Carlo?"

"Paragem, before I could get him."

"So you dropped Paragem off the cliff."

"Craylon did. We didn't need him anymore. Party's over. Last shipment goes out tomorrow . . . we split."

Carter backed away and motioned with the Galil. "Take me to Craylon and the woman."

Nikko's eyes worked like a cornered rat's, but they found no way out. He began to move along the wall, with Carter five paces behind him.

They bypassed the stone stairs down to the courtyard and went down a narrower set between the courtyard and the inner wall. A door at the bottom opened onto a well-appointed hallway.

There was a door on the right and another on the left.

"Which one, Nikko?"

"The left."

"Knock!"

He did and got an instant answer. "Yeah?"

"Nikko."

A chain dropped, and then the lock clicked.

The door was opened less than a foot when Nikko shouted a warning and threw himself at the opening. "Watch it, Myles! It's Carter . . ."

Carter was waiting for it and had the Galil on full auto.

He squeezed and kept squeezing as he threw himself through the door behind Nikko.

The tumblers stitched up one side of the man's back and down the other, sending the body rolling across the carpet. There was a solid trail of red in its wake.

When Carter was through the door, he sent his shoulder into Craylon's gut. The man lost a lot of air and landed five feet away on his butt.

He sat, wheezing, as Coco Chanette sailed through

what must have been the bedroom door.

She was a pro; one look told her everything, and she turned to split. Probably for an arsenal in the bedroom.

Carter sprayed the floor in front of her feet and brought her up short.

"On your feet, scum," he hissed at Craylon.

Laboriously the man gained his feet and followed the Galil's motion until he stood near the woman.

They made a pretty pair. Chanette was more mature than the photo Carter had, and hence more alluring. This wasn't hurt by a filmy peignoir and negligee set that hugged every curve of her body.

Craylon had movie-star good looks set off by the silver hair and a tall, muscular body.

"I don't suppose we could buy you off like we did Alvarez?" Her voice was calm, perfectly modulated, and her English was excellent.

"I don't think you could have bought off Alvarez," Carter replied, "if he had known the contents of the last shipment. He was an asshole, but I don't think he was *that* big an asshole."

Craylon spoke for the first time. "I have a villa, Carter, in the south of France. It's worth three million dollars. It's yours."

"And you can have the shipment," Chanette added.

"So you two can head back to Africa and whip up another one just like it? No way. Where is it? I figure about twenty kilos."

They exchanged looks.

Craylon broke first.

"It's loaded in the wine bottles on the carts in the courtyard."

"Damn you, Myles!" Coco Chanette hissed.

"All of it?" Carter asked.

"All but one kilo," Craylon replied. "That's in the bedroom."

"What was that one for?"

Another set of glances.

The Galil barked again, stitching a path in the carpet at their feet.

"The men—Nikko and the rest!" Craylon cried. "They're all junkies."

Carter felt sick to his stomach. "So you were going to poison them as a payoff? Jesus. Move, but not too fast."

The bedroom was small: one bed, a couple of lamps, and a table and chairs, with a half-eaten meal on the table.

An open bottle of wine was in the center.

"Get it!" Carter hissed.

Craylon did, from an open briefcase on the bed. Carter took the packet of white powder and set it on the table. Then he jacked the magazine from the Galil and leaned it against the door.

He would only need Wilhelmina now, just for the close work.

At the table, he cleaned the plates with the side of his hand, cracked the packet of heroin, and poured equal amounts on each plate. Then he poured two glasses of wine.

He motioned them into the chairs with the Luger.

Hate poured from the woman's eyes. Craylon, as he sat, wiped the sweat that dripped from his face.

"Eat it," Carter said.

"Jesus Christ, man!" Craylon gasped.

"He means it, Myles . . . don't you, Carter?"

"You bet your ass I do, lady."

"You're crazy!" Myles cried, his voice almost a squeak.

"Yeah, right now I am a little crazy. You see, Craylon, this is the dirtiest piece of crap I've seen come down in a long time. But to her, it's a job. To you? . . . shit!"

"But . . ."

"Eat it!" Carter hissed, grinding the muzzle of the Luger into Craylon's ear. "Eat it or buy it this way!"

Whimpering, Craylon picked up a spoon and filled it

with the deadly powder. It got to his lips but would go no farther.

Carter helped him out with the end of the gun, and Craylon washed it down with wine.

He gagged, but Carter held his cheeks and throat. Then came another spoonful, another, and yet another.

Craylon began to cry out in agony, holding his guts, with his pupils rolling back into his eyes.

Five spoonfuls later he was writhing like a stuck pig on the floor.

It took fifteen minutes for him to die.

Carter turned to the woman, but before he could speak she stood.

"I won't do it," she said.

"I didn't figure you would," Carter replied, flicking the Luger's safety off.

Chanette turned and started toward the bedroom door in calculated, measured steps.

Carter shot her twice in the back, severing her spine just as she reached the door.

He repackaged what was left of the white powder from the plates, picked up the Galil, and moved back down to the courtyard. At the gate he flashed his penlight three times.

From the ridge across from the castle, there were three answering flashes, and from somewhere far down the road, Carter heard a truck start up.

In no time he saw the lights, and minutes later Fernando and Lars pulled into the courtyard.

They asked nothing, only listened.

"You saw the one at the gate . . . there's another in there, in the cooking room. The other three are up in a bedroom on the second floor. You know what to do with the wine bottles."

"*Oui, mon ami,*" Fernando replied, looking as though he might be sick.

Carter walked the length of the road to where he had left

the BMW. He kicked it into life, and as he drove back to the villa, he went over the end in his mind.

The bottles would be buried. The bodies would be wrapped in canvas, weighted, and loaded aboard Fernando's boat. From there they would never be seen again.

Leonita met him at the door.

"Camilla?" he asked.

"Asleep."

She followed him in and watched as he wearily slumped across the sofa.

"Scotch?" she asked.

"A very tall one, neat," Carter replied, slowly rubbing his temples with the tips of his fingers.

"Is it over?"

"It's over. All over," Carter replied, standing and moving up behind her. He circled his arms around her beneath her breasts and pulled her toward him. "Two weeks?"

"Two weeks . . . three . . . a month. It doesn't matter. Just not here."

DON'T MISS THE NEXT NEW NICK CARTER SPY THRILLER

ZERO-HOUR STRIKE FORCE

Waddam moved much faster than Carter would have supposed possible, rolling over and reaching out for a telephone console beside the bed.

Carter lunged forward, bringing the barrel of the Luger across the man's fingers. Waddam cried out in pain; fell back and then looked up as Carter knelt on the bed, the Luger pressed against his skull.

"And now we will talk," Carter said in French, "about the *zero-hour strike force*."

"No!" Waddam screamed. He batted the Luger aside, and with a powerful thrust shoved Carter off the bed. He rolled the rest of the way over and grabbed the phone, but before he could bring it to his lips Avroix had come from the balcony, a silenced pistol in his hand. He fired one shot, blowing the back of Waddam's head off, blood, bits of bone and white tissue spraying up against the wall and the curtains.

Waddam flopped forward, knocking his face against the front of the console.

Avroix disengaged the telephone handset from beneath the dead man, and brought it to his ear.

Carter had picked himself up and he held the Luger loosely at his side. The safety, however, was off.

Avroix turned to him, the silenced pistol pointing in Carter's general direction. In the dim light Carter could see that the hammer was not cocked. It would take the man a crucial split second to cock the weapon before it would be ready to fire.

"You have caused very much trouble, Monsieur American intelligence agent," he said.

"I will kill you long before you fire your weapon, Avroix, please believe me," Carter said.

Something flashed in the man's eyes, and Carter started to bring up his Luger when Avroix's head snapped back, his right eye disappearing in a splash of blood at the same instant the sharp crack of an automatic came from the doorway.

Carter was around in a crouch, his Luger up, ready to fire before Avroix hit the floor.

Marie stood just within the doorway, her .380 Beretta in her right hand. She too stood in a crouch, a very slight smile creasing her lips.

"Jesus H. Christ," Carter swore half to himself.

He looked back at Avroix, but it was obvious the man was dead.

A siren started up below in the compound.

"Cover the door," Carter snapped.

Marie was halfway down the stairs when Carter emerged from Waddam's suite in a dead run, skidded and nearly tripped on the thick carpeting, then raced headlong down the stairs.

The guard from the gate burst through the front door, his rifle at the ready. . . .

**—From ZERO-HOUR STRIKE FORCE
A New Nick Carter Spy Thriller
From Charter in March**

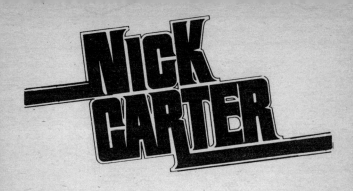

NICK CARTER

☐ 71539-7	**RETREAT FOR DEATH**	$2.50
☐ 75035-4	**THE SATAN TRAP**	$1.95
☐ 76347-2	**THE SIGN OF THE COBRA**	$2.25
☐ 77193-9	**THE SNAKE FLAG CONSPIRACY**	$2.25
☐ 77413-X	**SOLAR MENACE**	$2.50
☐ 79073-9	**THE STRONTIUM CODE**	$2.50
☐ 79077-1	**THE SUICIDE SEAT**	$2.25
☐ 81025-X	**TIME CLOCK OF DEATH**	$1.75
☐ 82407-2	**TRIPLE CROSS**	$1.95
☐ 82726-8	**TURKISH BLOODBATH**	$2.25
☐ 87192-5	**WAR FROM THE CLOUDS**	$2.25
☐ 01276-0	**THE ALGARVE AFFAIR**	$2.50
☐ 09157-1	**CARIBBEAN COUP**	$2.50
☐ 63424-9	**OPERATION SHARKBITE**	$2.50
☐ 95935-0	**ZERO-HOUR STRIKE FORCE**	$2.50

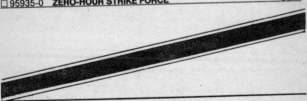

Available at your local bookstore or return this form to:

 CHARTER BOOKS
Book Mailing Service
P.O. Box 690, Rockville Centre, NY 11571

Please send me the titles checked above. I enclose _____ . Include 75¢ for postage and handling if one book is ordered; 25¢ per book for two or more not to exceed $1.75. California, Illinois, New York and Tennessee residents please add sales tax.

NAME _____

ADDRESS _____

CITY _____ STATE/ZIP _____

(allow six weeks for delivery.)

A8